THE BIG DRY

THE BIG DRY

A NOVEL

PATRICK DEAREN

FORT WORTH, TEXAS

Library of Congress Cataloging-in-Publication Data

Names: Dearen, Patrick, author.
Title: The big dry / Patrick Dearen.
Description: Fort Worth, Texas : TCU Press, 2024. | Includes bibliographical
  references. | Summary: "In this standalone sequel to The Big Drift-winner of five
  awards including the Spur Award of Western Writers of America-Patrick Dearen
  explores race relations against the backdrop of the Big Dry, a devastating drought
  in the 1880s in Texas. Zeke Boles, a Black cowhand, awaits hanging in North Texas
  for a murder he didn't commit. His white friend Will Brite, with whom he rode in
  the Big Drift blizzard, has exhausted virtually all avenues to get Zeke exonerated.
  Will's only hope is to set out for the faraway Devils River to find the actual culprit,
  a man with a missing finger. But Will has his own legal issues. He has married
  Jessie, a young woman of mixed race who often passes for white, and a grand jury
  is sure to return an indictment of miscegenation that could land Will in prison.
  Ride along with Will and his friend Arch Brannon as they join a cattle drive
  through a searing land between the Devils and Pecos rivers. This trail through a
  corner of hell is destined to be marked with carcasses and a lonely grave, but at its
  end lies the only hope for tomorrow"— Provided by publisher.
Identifiers: LCCN 2024032863 (print) | LCCN 2024032864 (ebook) |
  ISBN 9780875658872 (paperback) | ISBN 9780875658988 (ebook)
Subjects: LCSH: Texas—Fiction. | LCGFT: Western fiction. | Novels.
Classification: LCC PS3554.E1752 B544 2024 (print) | LCC PS3554.E1752 (ebook)
  | DDC 813/.54—dc23/eng/20240719
LC record available at https://lccn.loc.gov/2024032863
LC ebook record available at https://lccn.loc.gov/2024032864

TCU Box 298300
Fort Worth, Texas 76129
www.tcupress.com   *Design by Julie Rushing*

To all the readers of

The Big Drift

who asked for a sequel

CHAPTER 1

Jessie, Jessie! Have I wronged you?

Have I wronged you, sweet Jessie?

Thirty-year-old Will Brite had much on his mind as he stepped off his bay horse at the closed "whites only" tavern at Doans on the Texas side of the Big Red. Not only did everything about Jessie weigh on him, but somewhere there was a cowhand with a missing ring finger on his right hand.

Zeke Boles, a Black cattle drover facing the gallows in the shooting death of his employer and onetime master, had known it from the start. And now, Will knew it too as he mounted the creaking boardwalk. He had been here before, a half-dozen times in the fifteen months since a Texas Ranger had arrested Zeke far to the southwest. But in the sunrise light of this August day in 1886, Will saw the covered boardwalk as if for the first time.

The rays burnished a stain on the corner post, and Will ran his fingers down the smear. He could feel the texture of the wood's grain all the way to the boardwalk that still showed the dark blotch where cattleman Andrew Young had bled out and left Zeke seemingly culpable. Zeke claimed that he had been protecting the man who had been the one constant in his three decades, but in this unjust world, the word of a former slave carried little weight against the testimony of white witnesses. Indeed, seven Bar X drovers from the distant Nueces River had sworn to rushing from the tavern upon hearing the gunshot and finding Zeke alone, holding a smoking forty-five revolver over the body.

Will turned toward the sunrise. Off the far end of the boardwalk, the person truly responsible could have run away unseen by anyone else. As Zeke told it, a drunken cowhand had stumbled out of the tavern and found him waiting for Master Young. The intolerant cowhand had pistol-whipped Zeke, and when Young had come outside and defended Zeke, the assailant had gotten the best of him.

Every detail of Zeke's story made sense: With Young helpless against the post, the cowhand had cocked the forty-five to kill him, and Zeke had leaped into the fray. Zeke's finger had been on the trigger as they had struggled over the weapon, and when the revolver had boomed, Young had slid down the post and streaked it red.

Regardless of the truth, a white man like Will had died, and witnesses had seen a Negro with a grip on the forty-five. Zeke had been left with no choice but to run, and run he had—hundreds of miles down to the Slash Fives on the Middle Concho and into Will's life.

During Zeke's trial, there had been no way to establish his innocence, but Will had hope as he turned about. When he had visited Zeke in Wilbarger County Jail in nearby Vernon a day ago, Zeke had casually mentioned something not disclosed in court. The drunken cowboy's gloved hand had been over the muzzle during the struggle, and the bullet that had killed Master Young had shot off the cowhand's ring finger. Assuredly, when Zeke had rushed for his horse, he had seen a dozen chickens fighting over the prize just off the boardwalk and dislodging a thin gold band.

Now that Will had come in search, he found the ground between the boardwalk and hitching post dusty, for it had been heavily trafficked. Whenever rain had fallen, water had poured from the tavern's eaves and rendered the spot a mudhole. Boots had tramped or slogged through countless times, and any six-bits-a-day cowboy would have been drawn to a shiny article of value. The likelihood of finding evidence was remote, but Will retrieved a small shovel from the saddle of his horse and set to work.

As a buzzard wheeled overhead, periodically throwing a dark shadow across Will, he scraped and dug and sifted with his hands. He could hear the rasp of the shovel blade and smell the fresh dirt, but the only foreign objects that ran through his fingers were cigarette butts and old quids of tobacco. He was discouraged, and he used the side of his foot to scrape the excavated soil back in place.

When he tamped the loose dirt with the back of the shovel, he heard the ping of metal against metal and discovered a thin, gold band, just as Zeke had described. It was too large for a man's little finger, but a close fit for the digit alongside.

From the moment in the spring of '85 when Zeke had confided in him, Will had never doubted his account of the shooting. But there was something about holding tangible evidence that made it all the more convincing, and with spit and the tail of his linsey-woolsey shirt, Will cleaned and polished until the ring glinted in the sunlight. He couldn't wait to deliver it to Zeke's attorney, and as Will checked the location of the sun above the eaves of the tavern, he realized he needed to leave now if he was to keep their meeting at the Wilbarger County Jail.

With a glance back at the blood-stained boardwalk, Will mounted up and rode.

The county seat of Vernon lay sixteen miles south of Doans, and upon splashing his horse across the shallows of the Pease River two miles shy of town, he veered to the right across a broad bend covered in silver-seeded sage grass that brushed his stirrups. Beside a green mott of leafy pecans several hundred yards upriver, smoke rose from alongside a white wagon sheet that shone in the sun. Will had removed it from the bows of the nearby rickety wagon and stretched it as a shelter. The canvas was torn and leaked in a few places, and it rippled and popped in even a modest wind, but it had been home ever since he and Jessie had married.

Unnatural!

3

The word came to him suddenly and powerfully, convicting Will just as it had when the circuit rider had preached at the general roundup on the Pease in the spring. The matter had troubled Will ever since, for until the booming voice had carried through the cow camp, he had been unaware of not only man's law but of what God's law might be.

And yet Jessie meant so much to Will. After Zeke had rescued him from the fiery death he felt he had deserved, she had taken Will's hand and walked with him. Through all the long miles up to Wilbarger County with a handcuffed Zeke and the Texas Ranger, and on through more than a year of trying to save Zeke from a hangman's noose, Jessie had been at Will's side. She had helped him learn to forgive himself for his sins as a boy, and in so doing she had taught him how to live again.

But now judgment may have caught up with them both.

Will could smell the drifting wood smoke, and he veered a little so that he approached without throwing dust over camp. He came upon twenty-one-year-old Jessie stirring a large cast iron pot with a stick, much as he had found her doing the washing behind a shack on the faraway Devils River on the day when, in self-defense, he had killed the abusive man she had called Papa. From the start, Will's relationship with Jessie had been complicated by factors outside their control, and now their dark secret may have been exposed. If the grand jury indicted Will, he might face years in prison for no greater crime than loving Jessie enough to marry her.

It was man's law and man's punishment. But what of God's?

If anything was reassuring about the legal situation, it was that it would be Will alone, and not Jessie, who might be prosecuted. Even so, there was much to worry about, but for the moment, Zeke's fate was the more pressing concern.

"Look at this, Jessie," said Will, pulling rein and reaching into his shirt pocket.

The fire's hiss and the gurgle of the water must have muted the sound of his approach, because she seemed unaware as she looked up. But there was more than surprise in her face, for it held at once the striking features that had smitten him, and the subtle characteristics that might tear them apart.

Most enchanting were her eyes, as dark as her curls and a perfect complement to her delicately flattened nose and full lips. There was vigor in her natural tan, while her square chin, although dainty, suggested the strength of character that had led her to wrap him in her arms on the brink of perdition and promise never to let go. And all this in a five-foot-nothing frame draped by a simple cotton dress with a great bulge that made Will fear anew that he had wronged not only her but their coming child who would need the love and support of both a mother and a father. Jessie's time was fast approaching—any day now, from the looks of her.

He displayed the ring and set it gleaming in the noonday sun. "Down off the boardwalk, just like Zeke said."

"You found it. Will Brite, you *found* it!"

"Didn't think there was a chance in the world, but it backs up ever'thing he said."

"They've got to let him loose! Colored or not, this is enough for them not to hang him, don't you think?"

Will turned his hand over in a helpless gesture. "Can't help rememberin' what Zeke told me one time. Even if a white man caused the shootin', it's the colored one that will swing."

"You don't know that. Maybe when the appeals court hears about it . . ."

"Might be the only chance he's got," acknowledged Will.

"It's not fair."

"Neither is this other stuff."

The thick smoke, shifting with the wind, abruptly choked Will in a way it hadn't since the range fire on the Devils–Middle Concho divide. He had to turn away, but when he faced her again the soot still lingered in his throat like alkali dust.

"Never thought doings would get this far, the grand jury callin' me in tomorrow," he added. "Once Federson started the talk, I could've took you someplace where they don't know us. Then things got out of hand all at once, soon as that doctor let on that you couldn't handle a hard trip."

"*Doctor!*" Jessie repeated in disgust. "An old drunk like Papa, only worse. He didn't have any business spreading around his opinion. What's mixed blood got to do with him seeing me about the baby? We're not hurting anybody. Why can't they leave us alone?"

"I . . . I guess I've done you wrong, Jessie, marryin' you and all. I guess I hadn't learned all that much about what's right and wrong since I was ten and—"

"Don't you dare start that up again," she interrupted. "Don't you dare!"

Will didn't say more about his troubled boyhood. He might ride unflinching through a blizzard-induced mill of a thousand cattle with clashing horns and trampling hoofs, but he knew better than to cross her about an issue already settled, especially when she was in a delicate condition.

He glanced around at the sun. "I've got to start for town with this ring. Time I get to the jail, Zeke's attorney ought to be there. You need to go rest and quit tryin' to do so much."

He began to rein his horse about to leave, only to hear Jessie speak up.

"Will Brite, you wait a minute."

Laying the stick across the wash pot, she came up alongside. He removed his hat and leaned off the saddle to accept her outstretched arms, but as he drew her close with a hand to the back of her head and kissed her, the preacher's words came again, more damning than ever.

He separated us by races. He separated us, and we're to stay that way!

CHAPTER 2

It was like looking down into hell.

Wilbarger County had a new jail, but it was no more humane than the big hackberry on the courthouse square where authorities had chained Zeke when the Texas Ranger had escorted him into Vernon. A fourteen-by-eighteen-foot structure of hewn cottonwood logs, the jail was perpetually gloomy inside, for there were only two barred windows, each three feet long and six inches wide. Ventilation was an even greater issue on a summer day. The only access was by an outside staircase leading up to a trapdoor in a flat nook on the otherwise pitched roof that rose above it, and as the surly deputy with the tobacco-swollen jaw unlocked the trap and leaned it back with a squeak of hinges, Will could feel the hot air boil up as if from an oven.

He stepped aside and let the deputy drop a twelve-foot ladder inside, but just as Will started to climb down, a voice called from the shadows below.

"I'm coming up."

Will backed away and watched Zeke's attorney emerge, his flushed face perspiring profusely. The heavyset man was out of breath as he struggled off the ladder and spoke.

"Mr. Brite."

"You must've got here early," said Will. He turned to the deputy. "Can I talk to Mr. Smithson by myself?"

The deputy retrieved the ladder and locked the trapdoor. "Call me when you're ready to see the prisoner," he said, turning to the staircase.

Will watched him descend and then presented Smithson with the ring.

"Zeke never said nothin' about this till yesterday. He tell you about shootin' off that cowhand's finger?"

"No, he did not."

As beads rolled down the attorney's face, Will related the gist of Zeke's account and told how he had found the ring.

"Proves his story's on the up and up," Will concluded, more wishful than certain.

Smithson stirred the ring in a sweaty palm with his index finger. "No markings. Some people engrave their initials inside."

"It enough to get him a new trial at least?"

The lawyer continued to roll the gold band around in his palm. "I wish you had apprised me of your intentions, Mr. Brite. Provenance will be an issue."

"Prov—?" It was a word that made Will wish for Arch Brannon.

"Officers of the court should have been present. Otherwise, there's no way to establish the ring was found there."

"I never thought it would still be around after all this time." Will sank inside. "I . . . I'd hate to think it was my fault diggin' it up, when it might could've made the difference."

Smithson sucked on his teeth. "I'll be frank with you. He being colored and the deceased white, I doubt that anything but the eyewitness testimony of another white person could change things."

"So, we're just playin' out our hand then, waitin' for the rulin' to come back against him?"

"His execution is inevitable, I fear. I tried to make that clear from the beginning to the party who hired me for his defense."

Will studied his face. "Guess you still can't tell me who it is."

"I regret that I'm not privileged to do so. The circumstances are certainly unusual."

Will looked down with a deep sigh. "It's a awful thing, a innocent man fixin' to hang. From the start, he's accepted what's comin', but I can't."

Smithson must have read the despair in his voice. "From your interest in his case—that and the rumors from the district attorney's office—I perceive you may have special empathy for people with the curse of Ham."

Will looked up. "Curse of—?"

"The Negro race," explained Smithson.

"It's nobody's fault the life you're born to. Ever'body deserves the same chance, I figure."

Smithson tugged his earlobe as if pondering Will's words.

"An interesting perspective. Regardless, I want you to know I'll safeguard my client's rights to the very end. For what it's worth, I believe that he was indeed protecting Andrew Young from assault when the firearm discharged. But he did abscond with the gold coinage."

Will had all but forgotten about the funds from the sale of Young's herd. According to Zeke, Young had entrusted him to wear the money belt to foil would-be robbers, who would never have expected to find it on a black man. After the shooting, many miles had passed under the hoofs of Zeke's horse before he had remembered it.

"He never intended to keep it," said Will. "I was supposed to go bring it back, but between daywork and ever'thing else, I never have. He wants it to go to Andrew Young's widow."

"He indicated the same wishes to me."

"Don't guess that would make no difference, far as his hangin' goes?"

"It would be a kindly act, but not one that's likely to impact the appellate court." He looked at the ring in his palm and closed his hand around it. "I will, however, immediately notify the court of your find. Time is of the essence. We can expect the appeals process to conclude any day now."

"Wish there was somethin' I could do."

"You're very much your own man, Mr. Brite, unswayed by societal conventions or law. I wish you luck on both counts."

As Smithson's shoes tapped a cadence down the outside staircase, Will summoned the deputy. Soon, the trapdoor was open again and the ladder in place, but just as Will started to descend, the jailer snorted.

"Take quite a shine to colored people, don't you," he said.

Will turned and stared at him. "Zeke Boles has done more for me than any man alive."

"Won't do much for you now. Talk is, you'll be down there with him before long." He gave a crooked smile. "I'm saving you a place."

His words went with Will down every rung, and when he reached bottom and the jailer withdrew and closed the trap, everything seemed as dark as the Texarkana night before kerosene-induced flames had erupted and stolen away Will's boyhood innocence.

"That you, Mister Will?"

Will saw a figure stirring in the corner. "I swear, Zeke, you ever goin' to quit callin' me mister?"

"I tells myself not to, but it slip out, sure do."

Will went closer. "Even hotter in here today than yesterday." More than the heat made the air stifling; it reeked with sweat and urine and worse things. "You roped up the slop jar for emptyin' lately? What Arch calls a chamber pot?"

"Asked jailer man to, but he say this is what I gets for killin' a white man. Reckon he's right, sure 'nough."

"Even if it was your fault, which it wasn't, Andrew Young wouldn't have wanted it this way, from what you've told me."

"Best man I ever knowed, Master Young was. Heat don't bother me nohow. Feel awful good on what wigglers I got left in my boots."

Will had lost two toes to frostbite himself, thanks to the blizzard through which he, Zeke, and Arch Brannon had ridden when thousands of open range cattle had drifted south into Texas. When spring had come, the Big Drift had led to the largest roundup ever on the Devils River—and to all the events that had culminated with Zeke's pending execution and Will's potential prosecution.

"Zeke, I found that cowhand's ring."

Zeke didn't respond.

"Took a shovel over and dug around," continued Will. "Been buried up all this time."

Zeke persisted in his silence.

"Zeke, you've gone quiet on me."

"Bad memories, Will. Awful bad memories. I still sees Master Young bleedin' out."

"Yeah, guess we both know how things stay with a person. But I wish you'd quit blamin' yourself."

"Only finger on that trigger was mine when ol' six-shooter go off like hell a-poppin'. Own up to what you done, voice inside tell me. Take what you got comin', it say, so's I can show my face to Boss Man up high come Judgin' Day."

"I know what it means to you, makin' things right with the Almighty. But ever think maybe He's not ready for you yet? That you got things to do first?"

"Figure if I climb them steps and they puts ol' noose around my neck, it's supposed to be that way. If Boss Man want it different, He won't go lettin' it tightcn up."

"Maybe he wants you to help yourself, instead of waitin' for Him to do it. How come you never said nothin' about shootin' that cowhand's finger off?"

"Boss Man knowed I done it."

Will sighed and shook his head. "What else you hadn't ever told nobody? First thing your attorney did when I give him the ring was look for initials inside. If you want to talk about judgin', the man that was wearin' it has got a lot more to answer for than you ever will."

"Never did learn ABCs, but drunk cowhand sure 'nough scratched his two marks in the butt of that ol' Schofield six-gun."

"The revolver that went off and killed Young?"

"Right there in the wood, sure 'nough."

Will reached out and found Zeke's arm. "You're tellin' me he had his initials carved in it? My Lord, Zeke, why didn't you ever say something? Can you draw them for me?"

"That Schofield got hants all around it, is all I 'member. I expect they's still right there with it on the Slash Fives. Master Young's money belt too, all stuffed in a dead cow. Promise me again, Will. After they hang me, promise you's takin' that gold back to that poor woman sufferin' 'cause of me."

For now, however, Will wasn't concerned about Young's widow. On the contrary, he had a mission to consider, one in which every moment would be critical.

"Zeke, there's hundreds of dead cattle on the Slash Fives. Thousands. Tell me how I can find that carcass."

CHAPTER 3

The way Jessie's wind-blown dress hugged the contours of her abdomen was a troubling reminder of all they faced.

Will had seen her from a distance, lying on a cot under the shading wagon sheet, but as he had approached on his bay, she had struggled to her feet. For the last month, getting up on her own had become increasingly difficult. Now, breathing heavily from exertion, she stood with a hand on a corner support post, the hot gusts whipping her curls. For weeks, her cheeks had held a pleasant red tinge, almost a glow, which Will had supposed was natural for a woman in a family way. But he had never seen her this flushed, even though the afternoons had been oppressive all summer. When he reined up before her, the weariness in her voice was equally concerning.

"Tell me, Will Brite. I've been anxious ever since you left."

"You drinkin' plenty of water?" he asked as he dismounted.

"I was just going for some. What about the ring? What did the attorney say?"

Will hitched his horse to the nearby wagon wheel and went in under the first big pecan. On a crude stand, they kept a cedar water bucket in the shade, although the rays had worked through the rustling foliage and now glinted inside the rim. Removing a dipper from a nail in the tree, he found the cooler water toward the bottom and took it to her.

He stood watching her sip as the canvas overhead popped in the breeze. He felt a sudden need to place his hand on the bulge of new life inside her, and when he did so momentarily, she lowered the dipper, and they looked at one another.

"Jessie, tell me what to do. About you . . . about us . . . the grand jury. I tell you, I'm beside myself worryin' about it all."

Her eyes began to well. "Listen to me, Will Brite. We've got one more night. All I want is you to hold me. All night, just hold me. By the time the sun's up, you need to be gone. When the baby comes and I'm on my feet good, find someplace for us and send for me, like we said."

"They'll keep houndin' us, Jessie. No matter where we go, talk will start up again some way and they'll just keep after us. I done you wrong marryin' you, and didn't even know it."

"Just 'cause people make laws don't mean it's wrong. You know how it was. I was just drifting through life, you too, both of us dying more than living. Then I opened the door, and you were standing there the way it was meant to be."

"Meetin' each other's one thing," said Will. "Marryin' is somethin' else. I guess God's punishin' us for it, punishin' *me*, anyway. That preacher I was tellin' you about? He was goin' on about God puttin' people where they're supposed to be, settin' ever'body off to themselves by tribe and so forth. Boundaries, the preacher called it, lines we're not supposed to cross. Guess that's what I done, crossed a line, and some things can't be took back."

He glanced at her abdomen.

"Are you still listening?" she asked. "You and me were brought together, Will Brite. God doesn't make mistakes."

"I don't know, Jessie. I don't see how Zeke fixin' to get hung's not a mistake. Appeal court's goin' to rule any week now, and his attorney says the ring won't do no good. Soon as the judgment comes back against him like ever'body expects, all they'll be waitin' on is somebody buildin' the gallows and a judge signin' the hangin' order."

The color drained from Jessie's face. "Oh." For a moment, the pained word was all she could say.

"It's bad, bad as they come," added Will.

With a deep breath, Jessie seemed to draw on a reservoir of strength. "What we take for bad," she said quietly, "God takes for good."

"What good, Jessie?" Will pressed. "They're goin' to *hang* him."

"You said Zeke's never been at peace this way."

"He's made things right with the Almighty, sure enough."

"Then maybe that's it, that's the good."

"Thought I'd straightened things out with Him myself, till all this other stuff come up. Now I'm as tore up about what's right and wrong as I ever was." Will's eyes began to sting. "And this time I won't . . . I won't . . ."

His voice choked. "Lord, Jessie," he eventually managed, "I . . . I won't have you to take my hand and walk through it with me. Tell me, Jessie. Please tell me what to do."

She drew him close, and as he felt her curls against his cheek, she whispered words that he needed to hear.

"God's hand is a lot stronger than mine, Will Brite. It's stronger than anything life can throw at you. Don't ever forget that."

———

Will had seared every moment into his memory, for he didn't know if he would ever be with Jessie again.

With the cots drawn flush, he had held her all night, forcing himself to remain awake so he could relish the feel of her in his arms and hear her peaceful breathing as she slept. All too soon, day had begun to break, streaking the east sky red, and he had slipped out of their mutual embrace and saddled the bay. He had hoped to leave before she awakened, thinking it would be easier on them. But as he secured a pair of burlap bags to the saddle, one on either side, he wasn't disappointed when she came up beside him.

"It's been too quick," she said. "The time we've had, it's all been too quick."

He couldn't face her, not even when she put her arm around him and laid her head on his shoulder.

"I've got to make some miles, Jessie."

"Yes."

Never had the singing of crickets been this lonely, or the dawn broken so gray. Withdrawing, Will freed the reins from the wagon wheel. Taking the bay's mane in his left hand, he reached for the off side of the saddle and started to mount up, only to hesitate at Jessie's touch.

"Not yet," she pleaded.

Still, Will wouldn't let himself look at her. Maybe if he focused on the practical rather than the goodbyes, he could bear this better.

"Left you most of the pay. Don't figure I'll be needin' it." He twisted his fingers in the mane. "Got you enough wood and all the water I could haul up. Watch for rattlers in the woodpile. See any, kill them. Remember, that old revolver I bought shoots a little to the left. Watch that one mule when you go to hitchin' up the wagon. Don't want the thing to kick you and hurt you or the—"

Now Will did turn, searching the reflection of the glowing horizon in her eyes and wondering if he would ever see their child. Abruptly he shuddered, for he remembered that her mother had died in childbirth.

"How . . . How can I do this, Jessie? Go off and leave you when you're havin' so much trouble?"

"They'll take you away from me anyway. You know they will."

He knew, all right. For two years and maybe five, locked away in the penitentiary with the threat of more prison time if he and Jessie ever cohabitated again. The sheriff had made the criminal code plain when he had questioned Will about the accusation.

"I've got to go, Jessie. Jessie, I've got to go."

"Hold me," she whispered through emotion. "One more time, so I can remember."

It was the same thing she had asked of him back on the Devils River when other circumstances had threatened to wrench them apart. Now as she came into his embrace, he would have clung to her until they died in one another's arms, but the east sky was brightening and the punishment of man, and maybe God, was growing nearer.

Jessie's fingers lingered on his shoulder as he turned to the bay.

"I love you, Will Brite."

But Will's voice wouldn't work, and all he could do was place his hand on hers before he stepped up in the stirrup. Seating himself in the saddle, he hesitated for a moment, gathering his courage, and then he reined the horse away from Jessie and fled the injustice.

CHAPTER 4

The setting may have been the same, but the difference in details was stark.

On the day twenty months ago when Zeke had ridden into his life, the drift fence atop the divide just south of the Middle Concho had been sheathed in ice, and so had every scrub mesquite and tasajillo stalk. A bitterly cold wind, thick with ice pellets, had pushed out of the north sky's deep, ominous blue and rendered conditions all but unbearable for a man, especially one trapped under a horse in a tangle of barbed wire. Until Zeke had freed him, Will had been on his way to an early grave with only a cedar post with peeling bark as a marker, and now Will had come back to try to give Zeke, in turn, all the tomorrows that otherwise would be stolen away.

But while the posts alongside Will's nodding bay still marched west through the same broken country, the falling sun burned with a silent rage, glinting from the four barbed strands. Termite dust crusted the fallen twigs once glazed by ice, and with the bay's every pace, a haze rose up from barren ground that lay in sharp contrast to the snows of that awful winter. The numbing cold had burned Will's throat with each beleaguered breath, but the alkali that choked him today was almost as unpleasant.

Drouth had struck the Slash Fives, a terrible drouth that had left not a blade of grass. A lone jackrabbit couldn't have survived, and Will wondered what had become of the Slash Five herd that he and Zeke had chased after with Arch Brannon and Wampus. Still, he had greater worries, for two hundred sixty miles had passed under the hoofs of his bay since the Pease, and Zeke was a week closer to hanging.

And Jessie was that much closer to childbirth.

For more than an hour, Will had ridden past cattle carcasses, hundreds of them. Some were mere skeletons with horns and hoofs, for in the aftermath of the big die-up, he and Zeke had spent weeks skinning and shipping hides to San Angelo for the dollar apiece they had fetched for the Slash Fives. But for every hide harvested, a dozen others had been rendered worthless by the sharp talons and beaks of vultures. Left to fester in a broiling sun and another long winter, the remains still reeked and seethed with maggots.

Finding one carcass out of so many seemed daunting, but Zeke had explained that this cow had died four or five years ago rather than in the winter of '84–'85. Finally, Will rode upon a carcass marked by withered shreds of parchment drawn tightly across a collapsed rib cage. It stretched out almost flat, as though completely desiccated, with one horn upright and a rear leg raised and cocked.

Dismounting and snubbing his horse to a post, Will approached the carcass and nudged it with his boot, a way of inducing any hidden rattler to give warning. Reassured, he knelt and inserted his arm almost to the shoulder. Finding a loose coil, he withdrew a money belt, its leather stiff and its shifting contents clinking. He took only a moment to check, but enough twenty-dollar Liberty Head gold pieces flashed in the sun to buy an entire herd.

Breathless with anticipation, Will laid the belt aside and plunged his arm back under the shrunken hide. His fingers closed on scorching metal, but not so scorching that he couldn't bring out a Schofield revolver, the sunlight winking in its fluted cylinder. The seven-inch barrel had rusted in places, and the decomposing carcass had stained the walnut grip, but he used the tail of his linsey-woolsey shirt to clean the butt until he could distinguish two etched letters with peculiar wings.

MW.

He twisted the revolver in the sun and studied the letters from every angle. The Schofield represented real hope for Zeke, for the tavern in Doans had been filled with Bar X trail hands on the day of the shooting—and the Bar X range on the Nueces lay only three days' ride to southeast.

Will would have started for it now, but his bay was spent and the sun was sinking fast. Fastening the money belt around his waist under his shirt, he slipped the forty-five inside his outer belt and untied his horse. He needed to drop down to the Middle Concho and camp where his animal would have water, if not forage.

Will had stooped a little to straighten his stirrup when he was surprised by a voice from beyond the bay.

"I marvel at what I behold."

Will looked across the saddle. Framed between the horn and the cantle, a short, wiry rider of mid-thirties approached through rising dust stirred by his roan.

"Of all the fair knights of the range," added the rider, "leave it to Will Brite to show himself on the road to Jericho."

Will's morale immediately soared; he had ridden this dark road alone for too long. Until he chuckled, he thought he had forgotten how.

"Usin' words like that, you'll never sneak up on nobody," he said. "They'll know it's Arch Brannon for sure."

The rider brought his horse closer. "'Words are easy, like the wind,'" he quoted with his precise diction. "'Faithful friends are hard to find.' Well over a year, has it been?"

"Ever' bit of it."

When the man reined up on the other side of the bay, Will accepted his outstretched hand across the saddle.

"Where has fate taken my esteemed friend?" Arch asked.

"Been on quite a ride, Arch, I'll tell you. Me and Jessie and Zeke."

"Ah, Jessie, the most beauteous cherub ever to walk the Devils River. Or is it seraphim? Where is Miss Jessie?"

Will's spirits fell. *He might never see Jessie again, much less be allowed to hold her.*

"And our ebony friend Zeke?" continued Arch. "The three of you seemed to disappear simultaneously. Consider my chagrin when Wampus assumed your duties as wagon boss."

"Can't even imagine," said Will. "He still here on the Slash Fives?"

"No, and neither is anyone else."

"Except you," Will pointed out.

"Indeed, although I no longer ride under the auspices of that celebrated firm."

"You don't?"

"With the Slash Five's bounteous pay, I had hoped to prove the validity of the axiom 'a million days, a million dollars,' but my accumulated wealth fell considerably short."

"So who you workin' for? Don't figure you're out in this scorcher for the fun of it."

Arch glanced at the sun. "The flaming orb in the sky certainly denied the range the chance to nurture our bovine charges. When the New York stakeholders liquidated the herd, they no longer needed the services of cowhands. Fortunately, the stockman's association retained a rider to maintain its thirty miles of drift fence."

"Meanin' you."

"And a lonely job it is, riding fence by day and baching by night in the Slash Five line shack. And speaking of that twelve-by-fourteen hovel, it would be my honor to host you for the evening."

"I was fixin' to head down and camp on the river. Hadn't slept under a roof since last time I was here."

"Then the line shack will seem quite the palatial estate."

The alkali rose up gritty and bitter as they rode for the line camp across the Middle Concho. Working its way up Will's sleeves and down his collar, the dirt irritated his skin, and wherever he rubbed a spot, the itch grew only worse. This was a Big Dry unlike anything he had experienced, and it seemed to suck the life out of every living thing and replace it with something out of perdition.

Exactly as circumstances had done to Will's spirit.

From abreast on his left, Arch carried the conversation as the horses dropped off the high divide and approached the river's line of scattered pecans, the only suggestion of green anywhere except for beargrass and prickly pear. Will hadn't realized that he had lapsed into silent reflection until he heard his name called.

"I dare say," said Arch, "you're not much for discourse today."

Will found Arch a silhouette rising and falling against the sun with the roan's gait. "Guess you been talkin' and nobody listenin'."

"I admit I've had more stimulating conversations with this noble steed of mine. You seem to have much on your mind."

"Yeah."

Will faced the pecans again, and he was glad that Arch didn't say more.

Down inside the riverbank, they paused between a big pecan and a plum tangled with gooseberry vines and let the horses drink. The river was distressingly low, barely high enough to float a few lily pads, and the geldings struggled to draw up water between their pursed lips. It was plain to see that forage hadn't been the only issue in keeping a herd here.

"Never seen this country in such a shape," said Will, listening to the slurp as the horses drank. "Not even when we was skinnin' those dead cows."

"Indisputably," said Arch. He removed his sweat-stained hat and wiped his brow. "To paraphrase a dictum, 'one hundred miles to adequate water, seventy miles to a railroad, forty miles to a post office, and three inches to hell.'"

Hell.

Will knew all about it. He had lived it as a boy, and it had followed him for another nineteen years until Jessie and Zeke had helped him make peace with the Almighty. Now it had taken hold of his life again, in a way that had nothing to do with the vexing dust or the setting sun that reflected in the upstream shallows.

Two hundred yards past the river, they came to the line camp, which consisted of a weathered box-and-strip cabin, a west-side shed, and a two-acre trap. Will had spent a lot of days working out of this camp, and there was something comforting about the familiar surroundings. When he unsaddled his horse at the open-sided shed, the low eave brushed his hat as always, and an overhead sheet of loose tin banged in the wind just as before. After turning the animal into the adjacent trap, he followed Arch to the same stacked rocks at the shack's north-side door, and when he stepped up inside, the floor sagged and creaked as if welcoming home an old friend.

A friend was exactly what Will sought right now. It wasn't a cowboy's way—much less Will's—to bare his soul to another cowhand, but as Arch lighted the kerosene lamp on the rickety table across the single room, the small flame seemed to ignite Will's pent-up need to confide.

"Arch, Zeke's in a fix, and so am I."

Arch turned, and from his abrupt frown, he clearly realized that he should listen. Scooting out a rope-bottom chair with a rasp, he motioned for Will to do the same. Before Will did so, he pulled the Schofield from inside his belt and laid it between them on the corner of the table. The lamp light flickering on the barrel drew Will's gaze as he began to speak.

"Man got killed with this. They're about to hang Zeke for it up by the Big Red." He rotated the six-shooter so that the butt faced Arch. "What's scratched on there's the only chance I got of stoppin' it."

For long seconds, the burning wick hissed quietly. When Will looked up, he found Arch staring at the weapon as if processing what he had heard.

"You do have an abundance on your mind," Arch finally said. "I presume our colleague is innocent?"

"I'd stake my life on it." Will related Zeke's account of the shooting—and the sentence handed down after jurors had deliberated for just ten minutes. "Only thing he's guilty of is bein' colored."

"And protecting a man he valued so highly."

"Zeke sure looked up to him, I think."

Taking up the Schofield in both hands, Arch twisted the revolver before the smutty globe and paid special attention to the butt. "May I ask how you acquired it?"

Will told him about the carcass but omitted reference to the money belt. "He says the gun's got hants all over it."

"Christened in death and lodged in death, as it were, the revolver affirms that characterization."

Arch bent closer to the lamp and studied the butt even more carefully. Will leaned with him, tasting the kerosene fumes in the radiating heat.

"That's the man caused it," said Will, nodding to the initials. "I've got to put my loop on him 'fore it's too late. Wasn't nobody else in that tavern 'cept the Bar X's bunch from the Nueces."

"The Nueces is as bereft of forage, cattle, and cowhands as the Middle Concho, I'm told."

Will hadn't thought his spirits could sink lower, but they did, and he showed it with an exhausted sigh of resignation.

"Then Zeke's dead," he said, hanging his head. "Those Bar X's hands is scattered clean to kingdom come."

"I deduce that you cultivated a compelling kinship with our ebony friend."

"With all he's done for me, don't seem fair I can't do nothin' for him."

"Perhaps that isn't the case, Will," said Arch. "When I conferred with the association secretary, he indicated that the Bar X's relocated its cattle to Pecan Springs."

Will straightened. "On the Devils?"

"A place intimately familiar to you and me."

And to Jessie, thought Will, disheartened even as he regained hope for Zeke. Still, he had to focus on the one thing he might have the power to affect.

"First light, I'm headin' out," he said. "Way Zeke's attorney talked, they could start hammerin' the gallows anytime."

Arch checked the gun butt again. "*MW*, each letter with distinctive wings—miniature horseshoes, I would say," he mused. He placed the Schofield back on the table and faced Will. "You've committed to a challenging mission, considering the many cowhands known by a sobriquet."

"Sobri—? You're still spoutin' lingo I can't understand."

"Sobriquet. Nickname. Pie Face, Slew Foot, and such. Even Wampus, I would presume, who, with his curmudgeonly nature, presented me boundless opportunities for mirthful chiding. If sobriquets are the norm for the Bar X's, identifying *MW* may be daunting."

"Maybe not," said Will. "Forgot to tell you—he got his ring finger shot off his right hand when that gun went off."

"Indeed," said Arch, raising an eyebrow. "Let's hope the Bar X's comprises Texans who tie their catch-ropes 'hard and fast' to their saddle horns. Ropers from northerly climes are prone to 'dally, then tally.'"

Raising his hand, Arch wiggled his fingers, signifying the potential loss of digits in dallying, a quick twist of the lariat around the horn to stop a bolting animal.

"There's another disquieting matter," Arch added. "What are your intentions if you *do* distinguish him? He would never return with you of his own volition."

"I . . . I guess I never give it much thought," admitted Will.

Standing, Arch edged beyond the table and rummaged in the open shelves lined with airtights. When he came back, he had a cleaning rod with bristles, a small bottle of neatsfoot oil, and a chamois pouch jingling with cartridges.

"Linen rags and kerosene are on deposit in the corner," he said.

"Better than scrapin' it with my pocketknife," said Will.

"Indeed. It would behoove you to ensure the Schofield is facile. You may find yourself in need."

Will knew what he needed, and it wasn't a breech-loading revolver with which he couldn't have hit a bull broadside. But it was true that a firearm might be good to have, and he had left the Colt with Jessie. As he and Arch fell silent, he broke open the Schofield and set to work cleaning the bore and cylinder. The barrel was particularly challenging, and as he scrubbed the rust with a kerosene-doused rag, Arch spoke up.

"You've left me pondering, Will. The personal predicament to which you alluded—is there something else you want to disclose?"

But Will wouldn't look up. He had hinted at more, all right, but now he couldn't bring himself to talk about what he truly needed—the young woman denied him by man and maybe God.

———

It must have been all the dust hanging in the air.

Will had seen a lot of dawning skies as he had saddled a horse at the line camp shed, but never one this rich in color. As he readied the bay, it flared across the horizon, a fire painting the dark with twisted ribbons of red and yellow and orange. Maybe the sky held the promise of a new day, but it also gave Will the uncomfortable feeling that he was watching hell creep across this land.

Or maybe it already had. As Arch had told him, "The dearth of rain has forced even the aristocratic buzzard to bear a canteen."

Arch rode with him as they crossed the river and reached the drift fence. Will wasn't one for goodbyes—he constantly replayed the scene with Jessie—so he was glad when Arch's duties delayed their separation and they both turned left alongside the cedar posts. Even so, Will had little to say as they bore into the sunburst to the rhythmic beat of hoofs.

An hour after sunup, Will drew rein at sagging barbed wire between posts set the standard thirty-three feet apart. He needed to part ways and cross over, for a modest distance beyond lay the feeder draws for Spring and Dove creeks, where water holes marked the traditional staging ground for the dry push south-southwest to the Devils River. Upon dismounting and stamping down the loose strands, he was surprised to see Arch step his horse across with him.

"Workin' this side of the fence for a while?" Will asked.

"Under other circumstances, your assumption would be warranted. But I lay awake in the night considering the plight of our ebony friend. I am in greater debt to no other man."

"You and me both," said Will.

"From what Wampus described of my near-drowning, I owe Zeke my life."

Assuredly, when Arch's panicked horse had lost its footing and pinned him at the bottom of shallow Beaver Lake on the Devils, Zeke had dived underwater and freed him. Not only that, but after they had pulled Arch to shore and found him unresponsive, Zeke had taken steps to get him breathing again.

"A London physician named Silvester may have developed a method to induce respiration," continued Arch, "but I would have been consigned to an ignoble grave if not for Zeke employing it."

Ever since they had struck out from line camp, Will had been so caught up in his troubles that he hadn't noticed the floppy bedroll behind the cantle of Arch's saddle. Now as Will looked at it, he didn't have to ask, but he did anyway.

"So what are you sayin'?"

"Within the hour, we can achieve the tributaries of Spring Creek. Eighty miles beyond awaits the Devil River and an opportunity, perhaps, to make recompense to my Ethiopian rescuer."

"So what about your job fixin' fence?"

"No self-respecting cow would trod a range so barren. If she did, the other side of the fence would be just as unappealing."

Will took a look at the dry country that lay ahead for them. Whirlwinds danced in the distance, and Arch must have noticed as well.

"I left a note tendering my resignation at the line shack," Arch added. "My last duty will be to drive unspoiled staples into these posts. I want to discourage whirling manifestations of His Satanic Majesty from crossing back and forth at will."

"You mean dust devils?" asked Will.

"Isn't that what I indicated?"

As he had the day before, Will chuckled and surprised himself. "Arch," he said, "I'm glad you're goin' with me."

CHAPTER 5

It was like the valley of the shadow of death.

Back at the Pease roundup, the circuit-riding preacher had warned of a place of reckoning for anyone who violated God's boundaries between races. Maybe it was true and maybe it wasn't, but Will couldn't imagine a spot more fitting than the Devils River. All the way from the mudhole that now was Beaver Lake, he and Arch had seemed to ride under a dark cloud as the old mail road crossed and recrossed the intermittent stream down through the winding valley. For every pace of their horses, the stench of rotting flesh hung over them, burning Will's sinuses and roiling his stomach. Watched by buzzards that wheeled in a barren sky, cattle carcasses lay everywhere, clogging the rare pools, blocking the road, bunching against yellowing mesquites and sparsely leafed live oaks.

Maybe a blade of grass hid somewhere in the haze of dust, but Will hadn't found it in this land of the dead.

"Me and Zeke had a lot of talks about things," he said over the rap of hoofs. On his left, Arch's roan stayed abreast as they crossed the bone-white rocks of a dry ford just upstream of a sharp bend. "You know, what comes of somebody who does wrong and such."

"Are you speaking of the near term? Or ultimately?"

"After we're gone, I guess," said Will.

The horses flushed a half-dozen buzzards from a ripe carcass, and Will watched their winged shadow tracks crisscross the way ahead.

"Maybe a place like this," added Will, "is what a sorry SOB's got comin'."

"The Devils River would certainly be an apt metaphor," said Arch. "Or we can hope that our friend, the Bard of Avon, was prescient when he said 'He that dies pays all debts.'"

"You'd think dyin' would be enough. But supposin' it gets worse on the other side."

"For habitual grievous offenders, perhaps."

Will didn't like the sound of that. "That's just it, Arch. How many times you suppose we can be forgive? Say we get squared up with the Almighty about somethin', and then we start in kickin' against Him some other way?"

Arch pulled rein, inducing Will to do so as well, and the two men looked at one another.

"I confess," said Arch, "that my theological curiosity exceeds my theological wisdom. Are you grappling with a particular concern?"

Day and night from the Pease, Will had done exactly that, and his distress had grown a hundred times worse upon passing Beaver Lake and the nester's shack where he and Jessie had met—*Jessie*, without whom he was no longer complete. He yearned for her as never before, and yet with every pace of the bay, she grew more distant.

"I . . . I think I—"

Even Will wasn't sure what he was about to say to Arch before the words died in the squeal of a horse from ahead. A man hollered as well, a quick cry of alarm followed by a thud like the resonant first moment of a stampede. Will checked the ongoing road and exchanged glances with Arch, and then the two of them urged their mounts up the far bank of the ford. For dusty strides, they pushed across a bend, guided by a voice from the left-side brush that hid the river.

"You be all right, Tommy. You be all right, all right."

The phrase came again and again, and when Will's bay broke through cedar limbs tangled with elbow bush and mountain laurel, he saw sunlight reflecting in a pool past a riverbank freshly sloughed. He glimpsed a Hereford crossbreed knee-deep among festering carcasses in midstream, but it was the scene under the collapsed bank that seized his attention. A red dun horse was down and struggling to rise, and in the gravel and shallows sprawled a gangly man with tangled strawberry hair. He was passing a hand along his trouser leg and up his rib cage and spindly arm, obviously taking stock of his condition.

"You be all right, Tommy Blackburn; you be all right," he continued to assure himself.

"Are you sound?" asked Arch as he and Will pulled rein.

The man turned his head, and for an instant Will could see a freckled face with crossed eyes and a misshapen mouth. Then the rising dun with its dirt-coated saddle blocked Will's view.

"Ol' bank, she caved off with us, sure did," said the man.

Will took his bay a little to the left and stepped off so that he could see him again. Now the fallen rider, who appeared to be in his twenties, was coming to his feet.

"Not broke up are you?" Will asked.

The man rubbed his lower leg and continued to address himself. "You be all right, Tommy, sure 'nough all right." He retrieved a floppy hat, flapped it against his thigh as the dust flew, and put it on askew. Turning to the dun, he gripped the bridle and ran a hand down the horse's face. "Sure turned a cat, didn't you, ol' pony? You be all right, same as me."

"Horse don't look hurt any," said Will. "Lead him upstream a little and he can climb out easy."

As the man who called himself Tommy turned and spoke, a spray of saliva caught sunlight with his every word. "Got me a job to do, sure 'nough." He glanced at the Hereford crossbreed in the pool. "'Bring 'em in, Tommy,' Mr. Wash tells me. He rid on with first herd and leave me roundin' up."

He planted a scuffed boot in the stirrup.

"You with the Bar X's?" asked Will.

31

Tommy swung astride the red dun. "Mr. Wash my boss. Don't never want to ride for nobody but Mr. Wash."

"Wash? He the Bar X's boss?"

Tommy reined the dun toward the shallows. "Mr. Wash Baker, he be his own boss. 'Come ride for me,' he says. Nobody else wanted me, shufflin' me off one family to another. Mr. Wash sure treat me good, ever since I was fourteen. We's in the Davis Mountains now, me and him and Mrs. Wash and their little miss. He brung me with him on that SP train far as Comstock Station. Oh, what a hard ride it was on my horse gettin' here through Dead Man's Pass and all."

"The Bar X's wagon somewhere near here?" asked Will.

Tommy's red dun began wading out into the pool. "Pecan Springs. That's what they call it, Mr. Wash says, Pecan Springs. Mr. Wash headed for the Pecos right now. 'You round up second herd and bring 'em, Tommy,' he tells me. 'Cowhands of ours be meetin' us there and we'll take 'em rest of the way.' Eighteen hundred head of Bar X's stuff, Mr. Wash bought, sure did. Goin' across that ol' Pecos all the way to them Davis Mountains the cheap way. Won't pay for us to take 'em by rail, Mr. Wash says."

Tommy clearly had his challenges, but calming a shaken horse wasn't one of them. A bloody spot showed on the dun's shoulder, but he patted the animal on the neck and once more reassured it with gentle words. Dodging carcasses buzzing with flies, he circled the horse out past midstream to the crunch of underlying gravel and came up behind the Hereford crossbreed. For the first time, Will gave the bovine a close look, and the very word with which the circuit-riding preacher had condemned interracial marriage seemed to rock the Devils valley.

Unnatural!

It resembled a Hereford, all right, and yet it didn't. The cow had the familiar white face and dewlap of the breed, and, from what Will could see, the white underbelly as well. But this cow would have dwarfed an ordinary Hereford cross; if fully fleshed out, it could have carried sixteen hundred pounds. The forequarters, in particular, were uncharacteristically developed, and above the shoulders rose a peculiar hump. Even the color was distinctive: whereas a Hereford's coat was red and closely cropped in summer, this bovine was chestnut with thick, shaggy hair.

Overall, the cow was menacing in appearance, but it seemed as gentle as a blooded Hereford when the rider named Tommy began turning it out of the river.

"I swear, Arch," said Will, watching. "You got the education—what is that?"

"That, I believe, is what has earned the appellation of *cattalo*."

"Cattalo? What—"

"In this instance, the result of breeding a bull of the genus *bison*—buffalo, if you will—to a Hereford cow."

Will studied the animal more closely, picturing a Hereford alongside the buffalo he had once seen on the TX's at Horsehead Crossing. He recognized features of both, but this was a brute that would have been out of place in either bovine's world.

"Why'd they want to do that?" asked Will. Even as he spoke, he seemed to hear the preacher's booming voice again. *Some boundaries aren't to be crossed!*

"The concept," explained Arch, "is to generate a line of livestock with the prime attributes of both animals: the disease resistance and hardiness that allow a bison to thrive on scant pasturage and scarce water, and the docility and beef qualities of the Hereford."

"How come they're not ever'where then? Does crossin' them work that way?"

"That remains to be determined. It's my understanding that a Hereford cow, or Angus as the case may be, comes in calf only rarely when bred to a bison. And if the cow bears a male calf, she invariably dies of dropsy within a few months. Fertility in a surviving male is often in question as well."

Will shuddered, all his troubles overwhelming him. "Maybe . . . Maybe some things just wasn't meant to be."

"There does appear to be a lesson learned," agreed Arch. "We may insert our hand in nature's ways, but a toll might be levied to remind us of our folly."

Jessie!

Will's silent cry seemed to roll across the valley and stir his doubts again.

Have I wronged you, sweet Jessie?

CHAPTER 6

The past and the present merged until Will could barely tell them apart.

He and Arch rode alongside as the red-haired cowhand drove the cattalo down-canyon and repeatedly crossed the dry riverbed's snake-track course. During the roundup of the Big Drift herd in '85, Will had taken his horse under the strewn limestone of these very lechuguilla hills, and as the canyon now bent southwest, he relived the exhilarating days when a nester girl had brought to life feelings inside him that he hadn't known existed. A line shack door at Beaver Lake opened again and she stood there, a five-foot-nothing young woman with curls falling across her tanned cheeks. Those eyes, those captivating dark eyes . . . They held him in their grip, drawing him inside a soul as wistful as his.

Then with the canyon's westward swing on this day in 1886, he was at a wash pot fire behind the nester shack and brushing a gentle thumb across a bruise on her cheek—a mark levied by Caleb, the man who had raised her. Next the road of today veered north of west, and Will slipped tender arms around her for the first time and felt her tremble. At that moment, he had promised to hold Jessie, and to continue holding her, as long as she wanted—and now he may have ridden out of her life forever.

"My fellow knight of the range is in deep reverie, it appears."

At Arch's words, Will turned to his right. Approaching the Devils' westernmost bulge through shrubby, twelve-foot guajillos whose clustered limbs and lacy leaves hid the way, the three of them rode abreast, with Arch in the middle and the red-haired cowhand on the far side.

"Introductions are in process," continued Arch. "I've already bowed and tendered my name to our newfound acquaintance. I leave to you the honor of following suit."

Past the sweat-stained brim of Arch's hat, Will could see the younger rider's puzzled face. It was no wonder he was befuddled; Will himself could barely understand Arch sometimes.

"Name's Brite, go by Will," said Will. "Guessin' you're Tommy, from what we heard."

"Mr. Wash calls me Tommy, sure 'nough. Mrs. Wash and Little Miss too, eight year old. Awful nice to me, they is." Then he seemed crestfallen, for his lower lip pushed up. "'Round here, ever'body taken to callin' me Clabberhead."

Clabberhead. It was one of the things a cowboy might call a bronc that had little sense. Given Tommy's obvious handicap, Will didn't know how to respond to a nickname so insensitive, and even Arch was at a loss for words as they glanced at one another.

"Mr. Wash, he done rid on 'fore mean ol' cowhand started in on me," Tommy went on. "'Can't do nothin', can you, you clabberhead!' he tell me. They call him Rail, liken' to a fence rail, I reckon."

Will thought of Zeke and felt guilty. He may never have been rude to Zeke, but for a while Will had resented him because of his race.

"Next thing I knowed," added Tommy, "Rail's a-callin' me Clabberhead."

"He shouldn't ought to do that," said Will.

"Indeed, he should not," agreed Arch. "Mutual respect is as paramount to productivity on the range as it is in the House of Lords. A cowhand should mentor, not castigate."

"Arch is right, Tommy," said Will. "Most important thing in the cow business—any other, too, I suppose—is workin' hard and gettin' some confidence. Hard to believe in yourself when somebody's tearin' you down that way."

"It risks becoming a self-fulfilling prophecy," said Arch.

"Mr. Wash sure get mad if he knowed what Rail a-callin' me," said Tommy. "'You can do it, Tommy,' Mr. Wash keep sayin'. 'You can do it good as anybody.' That's how come him to leave me. 'Bring rest of them cattle to that ol' Pecos,' he says. 'You'll sure 'nough prove it to yourself you's good as anybody.'"

"A prime example of a mentor, I'd say," said Arch.

"From what you showed us back there," said Will, "I'd say he's taught you plenty already. You're sure good with that horse of yours."

The way Tommy beamed, twisted mouth and all, lifted Will's own spirits. Maybe boosting someone else's morale was just the salve he needed.

And then they broke through the densest guajillos and met a rawboned, dour-faced rider with crooked teeth and tobacco juice dribbling down his chin.

"So *there* you is," he snapped at Tommy as everyone drew rein. His voice had an annoying nasal whine. "You was told, 'Get cattle'—*cattle*, you clabberhead. Not that damned buffalo thing."

In a sage-dotted flat past the rider, who appeared to be in his late twenties, Will could see a roundup herd stirring dirt, the lattice-like leaves of intervening guajillos sifting the dust as it drifted and settled. Beyond the cattle loomed a four-hundred-foot rise with Spanish daggers. Through tall rushes near the escarpment's base, Will glimpsed the bright blue of a pool that meant a steady inflow of fresh water.

In a drouth like this, the lagoon was a refreshing sight, and at its lower end was the magnificent greenery of a pecan grove that gave the place its name: Pecan Springs. From this point downriver to the distant Rio Grande, as Will remembered it, the Devils was a living stream.

But where there was a river bearing such a name, there was the kind of person fit for the devil's own.

"Whatta you got to say for yourself, Clabberhead?" the cowhand demanded of Tommy.

Right or wrong, the rider had already made his point and now spoke out of plain meanness, thought Will. But Tommy defended his actions without flinching.

"Mr. Wash say he buy 'em all. He say, 'Tommy, they's ever' one ours now. You bring 'em in, Tommy, you bring 'em in.' That's sure 'nough the truth, Rail."

Will had already guessed that this was Rail. Even if he hadn't addressed Tommy by so disrespectful a name, the angular limbs and bony features would have been giveaways.

Rail spat a stream of tobacco juice that cut the dust beside the front hoof of Tommy's red dun. "'Mr. Wash, Mr. Wash,'" Rail mocked. "All you ever do is whine about 'Mr. Wash.' Knowed a clabberhead girl like you once. Didn't know when to keep her mouth shut about me. Have it your own way then. Throw the ugly critter in with the rest and git your butt to the wagon. Old man Ratcliff's wantin' a powwow with ever'body."

Not until Rail turned and slung his arm toward the pecan grove did Will notice that he wore gloves.

Gloves.

In the chill of winter, the men who rode for a brand might protect their hands, but seldom had Will come across someone who did so under a blazing sun. A cowboy lost too much dexterity in roping and other aspects of his job, and besides, gloves could be uncomfortably hot. Even now, sweat had soaked through and darkened the leather that outlined the rider's free hand. The other, his right, held the reins oddly between his thumb and his index and middle fingers, leaving the other digits stiff as if he avoided bending the two.

Maybe one of them couldn't bend.

Maybe the ring finger of the glove held nothing but stuffed grass.

Maybe *this* was the drunken cowhand in whose place a good man was about to swing at rope's end, his tongue sticking out and the blood vessels bursting in his bulging eyes. For torturous minutes, Zeke would dangle without dignity in front of gawking spectators, his trousers soiled by his evacuated bladder and bowels. The reflexive jerking of his limbs would hold everyone spellbound until a doctor eventually pronounced him dead, and it might be this very man—and not Zeke—who had been the cause of Andrew Young's killing.

Will had never wanted to shoot a man before, not even Caleb, Jessie's abusive father figure. But for a moment, the impulse was so powerful that Will was glad the Schofield revolver was stuffed in a burlap sack behind his thigh. A dead man couldn't answer for what had happened at Doans, not even a dead man with a missing digit.

Rail turned back straight in the saddle and rested both hands on the horn, the right above the left. Those fingers . . . those two stiff fingers that seemed unable to close. Maybe finding out the reason could come as easily as a handshake.

Will put out his hand, even though he would just as soon have offered it to a rattlesnake.

"Brite's my name," he said.

Rail looked at him but made no move to pump Will's arm.

"From the Slash Fives on the Middle Concho," Will added.

Will's hand stayed suspended, waiting for a handshake that didn't come.

"Broke two fingers ropin'," said Rail. "Near' jerked 'em off."

Was that a fleeting, downturned mouth Will saw? Followed by a self-satisfied smile? A sign of lying and then of enjoying the lie?

Will wished he knew, but all he could do was withdraw his hand.

Arch, however, was just as aware of how critical every moment was, and he tried a ruse of his own.

"*Rail*—I do say that's quite a sobriquet. Or, as an author would have it, a nom de plume. I'm Arch Brannon, from out of Galveston by way of the elite schools of England and the buffalo range. Sobriquets aside, whom do I have the pleasure of addressing?"

Let it be initials MW! Will pleaded silently.

But Rail, for the moment, only seemed confused, for he tilted his head and his brow furrowed. "Huh?"

"Your actual name," simplified Arch.

Rail flushed and his jaw tightened, both signs of anger. Too much anger, thought Will, for someone with nothing to hide.

Rail wheeled his horse toward the herd and loped the animal away. "Ain't somethin' you ask a man," he protested over his shoulder before he was out of earshot.

Will already knew it. *All I ask of a man is a hard day's work*, Slash Five manager Major Hyler had said not long before he had died in the Big Drift snows. Will had adopted it as sound advice, but that had been before he had left Zeke in a hellhole awaiting the gallows.

Will rode on with Arch and Tommy, the cattalo surging ahead in a powerful gait as its muscular hindquarters worked. Will had never seen a bovine with a stride so lengthy; even at an unhurried pace, the legs ate up ground in a hurry. He looked down the animal's lengthy back, considered the deep rib cage, and figured those two character-istics alone could yield an extra 150 pounds of meat at butchering. But that hump on its shoulders was so . . .

There was only one word that would fit—*unnatural*—and Will didn't even want to ponder it.

Riding guard over the roundup beeves were two cowhands, and Rail stopped and engaged the nearer in brief conversation before con-tinuing on around the herd. As Will came up behind the first guard, he recognized the slouching posture, but at the same time he was struck by a deformity under the sweat-stained hat brim. Flush above the jawbone, at a place where an earlobe should have been, was only a scar. In fact, all the cartilage that rimmed a normal ear was gone, leaving only disfigured tissue around the canal.

Frostbite in December, amputate in June.

Arch's long-ago words were unforgettable as Will spoke to the unaware rider. "Guess I'm not the only one got branded by that blizzard."

The cowhand drew rein and turned. A year older than Will, he was a stocky man with bulging veins in his temples and wild, bloodshot eyes. His perpetually flushed face, apparent even with dust clinging to his stubble, added to the suggestion of someone itching to fight. But Wampus was all bark and no bite.

"Alas and alack," said Arch, reining up with Will. "I misplace a toe or three—Will as well, I presume—and inconsiderate Nature has absconded with fair Wampus's ear."

Wampus snorted. "I can still hear *you* smartin' off, you and them fancy words."

"Ah, words," retorted Arch, "vital elements to convey thought from soul to soul."

Wampus grumbled unintelligibly before adding, "What I'd give to hear you speak English for once." Then he looked at Will. "Where'd you run off to last year? A man don't leave a job the way you done."

Or a sickly wife who carries his child, thought Will.

"You and that colored boy disappeared same time," Wampus went on. "Good thing I was around to run the wagon in these parts."

"And with his excellency Wampus in charge," interjected Arch, "we *still* managed to round up our noble bovine charges."

"Smooth as a horse cuttin' a tomcat out of a stovepipe," agreed Wampus.

Back in their Slash Five days, Arch had used so lofty a vocabulary to tease Wampus—*hooraw* him, in range terms—that Wampus hadn't always realized that he was the target of an insult. Clearly, things hadn't changed.

"Yeah," said Wampus, turning to Will again, "a man with any self-respect don't just quit on a job when they's work to be did."

"He does if he's got reason enough to," said Will. Indeed, it had been the same cause that still drove him—Zeke's life.

"That was a Slash Fives horse you taken, case you forgot," Wampus added.

"Never drawed my last pay. Figured it was a even trade." Will smoothed his hand down the bay's neck. "Besides, I brought him back."

Wampus studied the horse. "Yeah? All rid down, looks to me like."

Arch chuckled. "A sage poet once opined that if complaints constituted dollars, Lord Wampus would be a millionaire."

"Think I been ridin' with that poet the last few days," said Will.

Then Wampus found another matter to complain about. He focused on something behind Arch and sneered, and when Will checked, he saw Tommy turn the cattalo in with the herd.

"There's that clabberhead," Wampus groused.

Will faced Wampus again. With Rail—a complete stranger who now pulled up alongside the farther guard—Will had held his tongue. But Wampus had holed up with Will in the same line shack for months in '84, and later had taken orders from Will in the Devils roundup of '85.

"Name's Tommy," said Will. "No need callin' him nothin' else."

Wampus's face swelled like a mad horned toad. "Who went and made *you* straw boss? Kid's just dead weight 'round here."

"He's doin' the best he can, I imagine. No reason to make a kick about it."

"Clabberhead ought to git home to Mama. All he's good for."

"Hear ye, hear ye, the words of our Earl of Wisdom," said Arch. "Wampus is as adept at judging a person's worth as he is at managing a roundup."

"Know my stuff, all right," said Wampus.

Will decided to let the matter go for now. Men were just like horses: there were good ones, mean ones, and sorry ones. Wampus was just a step above sorry.

"Got powders to get to the wagon," said Wampus. "Them bony cows wander off ain't *my* fault."

As Wampus rode away, Will took a moment to study the herd. Wampus was seldom right about anything, but his description of the herd was on the money. Even in the Big Drift roundup, Will had never seen cattle so bereft of flesh. Sunken places outlined the bones to the point that a laundress could have used almost any rib cage as a washboard. Considering all the hairless places he took in at a glance, mange must have afflicted half the herd.

Only fifteen or twenty animals seemed healthy and in good shape, and when Will looked more closely, he realized that they, too, were cattalos. But unlike the cow that Tommy had driven back, these seemed less buffalo and more range stock, maybe bred through enough generations until they were 25 percent buffalo and 75 percent Hereford.

But they were no less unnatural, and Will worried anew what his and Jessie's child would face in a world in which a person's place was fixed by the races of great-grandparents long dead.

As Tommy rode past on the way to the chuck wagon just outside the pecan grove, Will caught movement across the herd and saw the other guard and Rail start for camp as well.

"Got to see what's in that glove, Arch."

"Indeed."

"Short of hog-tying him, I don't know how. But if we can catch him alone, I'll sure do it for Zeke if I got to."

"I know the time constraints Zeke is under," said Arch, "but it would behoove us to see if he removes it voluntarily. Meanwhile, we could inspect the other Bar X employees for the proper missing digit."

"Yeah." Will watched Rail ride away. "One way or another, I'm findin' out what he's hidin' that he don't want nobody to know."

"As the distinguished man of English letters Samuel Johnson wrote, 'Where secrecy or mystery begins, vice or roguery is not far off.'"

Will looked at Arch. They had both worked on the Slash Fives, all right, but out of different line camps, and even though Will counted him as a friend, he didn't really know him all that well. The week's growth of beard, the trail dust, the sweat-darkened getup no different from any other cowhand—they seemed so out of place on a man who expressed himself in terms a schoolmarm would have scratched her head over.

"What you was sayin' back there," said Will. "You really get your schoolin' in England?"

"My education was equal parts the finest schools of London, the lowliest buffalo-skinning outfit on the Sweetwater, and the most bedraggled company of rangers in the Sierra Diablo snows."

"I swan, Arch, never knowed anybody like you."

"There have been times my ilk would have repulsed you. I confess to periods of obtrusiveness, resistance, and general obstinacy—all stemming from unresolved childhood trauma."

You too?

His question unspoken, Will stared as Arch rode on toward the chuck wagon. Will may not have understood all the words his friend had used, but they had been powerful enough to raise troubling memories of his own boyhood—until he heard Jessie's admonition again.

Don't you dare start that up again! Don't you dare!

Jessie.

How could he go on without her, even for a moment?

Lost in thought as he followed Arch, Will abruptly found himself nearing the chuck wagon, its four bows bared like the rib cages of a thousand maggot-ridden carcasses he had passed in the Devils country. The camp, set against big, shady pecans, had a familiarity about it, even though the Bar X's hadn't been involved in the Devils roundup of '85.

As was typical, the extended wagon tongue on the left angled down to the ground, the harnesses draped across the doubletree and singletree. At the wagon's rear end, the upright chuck box was open, its door swung down to form a countertop supported by a prop stick. Steam rose from a coffee pot on a fire smoldering nearby, while bedrolls lay about camp, most of them in the open but a few showing inside the grove past the wagon tongue.

Will did as Arch and gauged the wind before veering to the right where other horses were hitched to underbrush. If there was anything that would rile the *cocinero*, or cook, it was someone riding in and throwing dust. The *cocinero* was busy stirring batter at the chuck box, but six or seven cowhands were gathering before a lean, almost frail man with gray hair at the rear wagon wheel. His soft voice, heavy with the flavor of the South, had already captured everyone's attention by the time Will tied his bay to a mountain laurel and approached with Arch to the smell of wood smoke and coffee.

"Boys, we've got a drive through hell coming." Showing plenty of years in his scored and ruddy face, he must have been old man Ratcliff. "Not a place I ever expected to be going back to. Been dodging it—Howard's Well, at least—most of my life." He developed a tic in his cheek. "But come daybreak, we're starting for Howard's and on to the Pecos. In this drouth, I don't see how man, cow, or horse can make it. No telling what's happened to that bunch ahead of us."

As Ratcliff spoke, Will casually moved through the crowd, checking hands and digits. No one but Rail wore gloves, and Will saw a few bent fingers but no missing ones or familiar faces from the witnesses at Zeke's trial. Arch stirred about as well, clearly on the same mission for a maimed hand.

45

Ratcliff withdrew the makings from his linsey-woolsey shirt and set about rolling a cigarette as he continued.

"If it wasn't for the stakeholders selling the Bar X's stuff to Wash Baker out in the Davis Mountains, we wouldn't be doing this." He sprinkled tobacco across a wisp of paper. "I'm telling every one of you like it is. From the time we leave the springs here, we've got a drive of nearly a hundred miles to the Pecos. It's our responsibility to get them that far and turn them over to Baker's men. With Beaver Lake a mudhole, not a drop of water till halfway or more, at Howard's Well."

Ratcliff's tic grew worse when he said *Howard's* again. "They say there's fifteen hundred miles of old road between San Antone and the Pacific, and not a longer dry stretch anywhere on it. Weak as those cows are, we have to ease them along slow. In this kind of heat, we'll be rationing water, but we just have the one barrel and it dripping all the time."

He nodded to the banded barrel riding between the wheels and then licked the edge of his cigarette paper.

"You boys hired on to work cattle, and I'm proud of the job you've done. But we're facing something you haven't seen the like of. With the men that went with the first herd, we're short of drovers, and I need your help. But you can quit right now, and I won't hold it against you."

Hanging the rolled cigarette in the corner of his mouth, he struck a match on the adjacent iron tire and lighted it.

Cowhands looked at one another. Will noticed one man's lips part, but words remained unvoiced. Finally, a hefty cowhand spoke up.

"Mr. Ratcliff, I expect ain't a one of us ever turned their backs on a herd. You know it good as anybody—owners theirselves would give up on a herd 'fore most any hand would."

Will had heard Arch put it into terms that only Arch would have used: *The responsibility of a cowhand to his bovine charges is beyond reproach.* In riding after the Slash Five herd that had drifted with the great blizzard, Will had displayed that kind of accountability and seen it in others. A good man had died in the snows, and other Slash Five hands had paid lesser prices in snow blindness and frostbite. But like Will, all of them had been driven in part by a work ethic that had placed their obligation to a dumb brute with a Slash Five brand above almost anything. For a six-bits-a-day cowboy who knew no other way to live, it was something to take pride in.

But there was always someone who didn't measure up.

"Ain't drawed no pay since we moved off of the Nueces," spoke up Rail. "What's it been, four, five months? I ain't in this for the fun of it."

"You'd just have gambled it all away," said the hefty cowhand. "No place to spend it out here."

Rail breathed sharply. "Ain't talking to you, fat boy. Ought to be mine to use any way I want to."

"Stick with me, if you're a mind," said Ratcliff. Every word came with a puff of cigarette smoke. "Soon as we deliver this last Bar X's stuff to the Pecos, I'm collecting cash dollars from Wash Baker for every head that makes it. You'll get your pay on the spot, same as the ones ahead of us."

When Ratcliff went quiet and there were no other protests, the cowhands dispersed, leaving only Will and Arch.

Ratcliff made eye contact. "You men looking? Sure could use you."

Will checked Arch through the drifting smoke. No cowhand had appeared to be maimed, but that pair of stiff fingers in Rail's glove seemed as suspicious as ever. Not only that, but the rest of the Bar X drovers, with or without ring fingers, would be waiting at the Pecos for their pay.

When Arch gave a nod, Will approached Ratcliff with his hand outstretched.

"Name's Will Brite," he said, feeling Ratcliff's firm grip. "Come daybreak, we'll be ready to ride."

All through supper and on into dusk, Tommy muttered to himself as he sat alone on the wagon tongue, a cow camp's designated place for outcasts like Zeke. Even after taking his dirty dishes to the roundup pan beside the chuck box, Tommy returned to the tongue and mumbled as he rocked and gestured.

Meanwhile, Will seldom took his eyes off Rail.

He watched the gloved fingers cut fried steak with a pocketknife and bring bite-sized pieces to his mouth. He saw the grimy leather sop sourdough biscuits in grease and spoon up the juice of canned tomatoes. After Rail sneezed and wiped mucous from his nose with the side of his forefinger, the wet glove still stayed in place. Just as striking was the unusual daintiness with which the thumb and first two fingers took up a tin cup of steaming coffee and tilted it to cautious lips.

And always, the ring and little fingers stayed rigid, flaring to the side.

For a while, Will sat with Arch at their bedrolls back under a big pecan, a position from which he could look out past Tommy's shoulder and watch Rail squat on his heels and eat. But as night gradually crept across camp and details began to fade, Will and Arch joined Tommy on the splintery wagon tongue to get closer. Nevertheless, once Rail finished supper and set about straightening his bedroll, his hands remained covered.

Tommy, immediately on Will's left, seemed unaware that he was no longer alone. He continued to rock and gesture and mumble, but now Will could make out much of what he said.

"Poor Mr. Wash, he done in trouble. Poor Mr. Wash . . . Poor Mr. Wash . . ."

Will traded glances with Arch. It was troubling enough for Tommy to sit on the wagon tongue apart from everyone, but his distress was apparently due to another matter. With someone who seemed a child in a man's body, Will didn't know how to broach the issues except with a cowboy's straightforward honesty.

"Tommy, how come you sittin' here on the tongue like you are?"

The slow-witted redhead seemed not to have heard, for he continued to rock and talk to himself.

"Somebody tell you to sit here?" Will pressed.

Now Tommy looked at him. "First night Mr. Wash gone, Rail say, 'Git your butt over there and sit, Clabberhead!'"

"Shouldn't've listened to him."

"Figured one mean man enough. Don't need no more. 'Do like he say, Tommy,' I tells myself. One mean man enough. Don't need no more."

"There somebody else?"

Tommy grew agitated, bouncing on the tongue. "One mean man enough. Don't need no more."

"Tell you what," said Will. "Now on, you come sit with me and Arch."

Tommy calmed a little. "You mean it? I don't got to sit here by myself? You mean it?"

"Course I do."

"Indeed," spoke up Arch. "We would welcome the company of so fine an equestrian."

Even in the shadows, Will could see Tommy squint in confusion.

"Arch means you're good with horses," translated Will.

"I do say," said Arch with a chuckle, "there seems an echo in this valley."

Will continued to focus on Tommy. "How come you takin' on so?"

Will almost wished he hadn't asked, for the young man grew upset again and began to shake his head repeatedly.

"Poor Mr. Wash, he done in trouble. Old Mr. Ratcliff say it, 'Don't see how nobody can make it.' It worser than Mr. Ratcliff know. Poor Mr. Wash."

"Are we to assume Wash Baker is an accomplished cowman?" posed Arch.

"Smartest man I ever knowed, Mr. Wash is," said Tommy. "Bestest one too. Poor Mr. Wash."

"Then I'll bet he's all right," said Will. "Few days, we'll catch up with him on the Pecos."

Tommy bounced and flailed his arms. "Be too late, too late. Mr. Wash done in trouble. Mean man, awful mean man."

Will caught movement out of the corner of his eye. He saw Rail stretch out on his side on his bedroll and roll a smoke. When he lighted the cigarette, the flaring match still showed a gloved hand.

"I says to myself, 'Say somethin', Tommy. You got to tell Mr. Wash, you just got to.'"

Will turned back to Tommy. "Tell him what?"

"Mr. Wash on point, his back always turned. Poor Mr. Wash done in trouble."

"I would wager," said Arch, "that there's little reason for concern about so exemplary a cowman."

But Tommy remained inconsolable. "Poor Mrs. Wash—Little Miss too, eight year old. Somethin' happen, they just be a-cryin' and a-cryin'."

"Tommy, you're talkin' in riddles," said Will.

"Be all my fault, not sayin' somethin'. 'Tell him, Tommy,' I tells myself. 'Mean man, awful mean man.'"

Will tried one last time to get him to explain, but now Tommy sprang up. Waving his arms, he stalked away into the dark, still muttering to himself.

CHAPTER 7

He came riding out of the south, a lone figure dancing in the heat waves as the late afternoon sun winked in his badge.

All day, through tears that wouldn't stop, Jessie had alternately written in a tally book—a letter that Will would never see—and watched for such a rider to approach her camp through the silver-seeded sage grass. Now as she stood holding to the corner support for the flapping wagon sheet, he seemed like one of the four horsemen of the Apocalypse in the scorched Bible that had been her mother's. Conquest, War, Famine, even Death—they all had seemed preferable to the moment when Will had ridden away, melding into the shadows from which he might never return to her. Then the baby had kicked, reminding Jessie of another life that God was knitting inside her, and she had once more found what she had never known before Will.

Hope.

Pocketing the tally book and pencil, she listened to the rhythmic strike of hoofs and growing creak of saddle leather and then he reined up before her, a mustachioed rider whose deeply scored face showed no concern that he had thrown dust across camp. Never had it tasted so bitter, and Jessie turned away to let the wind carry it on. When she again faced the man she recognized as Lem Hutchins, Wilbarger County sheriff, he slid his hand under his suspender and withdrew a document from his linsey-woolsey shirt.

"Got a writ of attachment for him," said Hutchins, unfolding the paper with a rustle. Looking up, he must have read the confusion in

Jessie's face. "Somebody dodge a grand jury summons, this is what happens."

Jessie only looked at him.

"District court issues a writ authorizing me to arrest him and get him there," he continued. "Twenty 'good, intelligent, and practical' jurymen, like the law says, got a right to hear him."

Lifting his squinting eyes, he seemed to scan the camp. "Where is he?"

"He's gone."

Hutchins's gray mustache twitched as he made eye contact again. "When he be back?"

"He . . . He's never coming back." The halting words came painfully, and Jessie couldn't believe she had spoken them.

The sheriff breathed sharply and picked at his flaring mustache. "Run off, did he? Well, I guess that answers that. What the district attorney calls a 'consciousness of guilt.' His name will look right good in the governor's next *List of Fugitives from Justice*."

Jessie's eyes began to sting and her voice grew even more strained. "Why—Why can't you . . . can't you let us be?"

"He passed up a chance to defend himself. Had a right to face his accusers."

"That old drunk of a doctor?"

For a moment, Jessie was back in the physician's upstairs office as a framed Hippocratic Oath on the wall rattled in a breeze from the window. She remembered one part in particular, something like "Whatever, in connection with my professional practice, I see or hear, which ought not to be spoken, I will not divulge."

Jessie thought of it another way: *I won't tell what should be kept private.*

"I went to see him about the baby," she said. "What call *he* have to go talking about me?"

"Doctor says coloreds has got things about them can't be hid, even

52

down three or four generations. There's Federson too. Seems to know a lot about your upbringing."

Jessie flinched at the mere mention of the name. She had heard the story from childhood on the farm in East Texas, how Caleb—the only father she had ever known—had enlisted Federson and other white men in tracking down a Negro who had raped Jessie's fair-haired mother. Several months after the men hung the Negro from a hickory tree, Jessie was born, at the price of her mother's life, embittering an already bitter Caleb. Jessie spent most of her years not knowing the full story, but in a drunken stupor one night, Caleb let slip that no forcible violation had occurred.

Jessie supposed that no one else knew the full truth, but Federson, a sharecropping partner of Caleb's, inferred enough to call her "Little Pickaninny" anytime Caleb was out of earshot. When Jessie turned fifteen, mature in body if not in years, Federson counted out cash dollars to Caleb and wagoned her away. For a month, Federson kept his distance from her, but when his words turned suggestive, Jessie fled for home. Meanwhile, Caleb had gone on a spree and spent every last cent, and before Federson could show up at the cabin and demand his money back, Caleb left with Jessie and eventually drifted to the Devils River.

Then, only a few months ago, Jessie came face to face with Federson on a dusty Vernon street. When the old devil learned that Caleb was dead and that the debt could never be squared, Federson's features went dark. Apparently deciding to take his revenge on Jessie, he had proceeded to spread stories that he had no right to tell.

Hutchins slipped the writ back in his shirt pocket. "Not much of a man, is he, this Will Brite." His focus seemed to drop momentarily to her abdomen. "Fornicate, flaunt the law, now run off and leave you when you's in this kind of way."

"You'd be carrying him off anyway. You said yourself. He . . . He's the kindest—"

Jessie might as well never have responded.

"No, not much of a man," interrupted the sheriff.

He started to rein his horse about before hesitating and raising an eyebrow. "I'll say one thing, though. Most places, you sure could pass for white. Good thing the truth come out, here in *my* county. It's damned depraved, the two of you. By the letter of the '79 law, the grand jury ought to indict you too. If it was the other way around, him colored and you white, you can bet they'd do it."

Through an uncaring world blurrier than ever, Jessie watched him ride away, on her lips a whispered prayer for Will and their baby who would always be caught between white and Black.

———

Zeke had been sentenced to hang, and he had only one regret.

Vennie.

They were supposed to be married by now. Upon his return to the Texas Gulf Coast after the Kansas cattle drive in '84, Zeke was to have plighted a troth holy in the Almighty's eyes. Master Young, the finest man Zeke had ever known, had intended to stand in witness as Zeke wed this colored daughter of Young's favored sharecropper. Mistress Young, the poor woman Zeke had widowed when the revolver had gone off in the struggle, would have been there as well. So highly did she think of Vennie that, just as Zeke had ridden away, she had promised to take Vennie under wing as her personal servant and afford her all the fineries of the Young household. Master and Mistress were to have built them their own home on the grounds, but all of that had ended when a Schofield had roared and forever stained a boardwalk with blood.

Vennie hated Zeke. She must have hated him as much as Mistress Young did, as much as Zeke hated himself. When the news had come, the widow and Vennie had no doubt wailed their grief, and grief had given way to a hatred that Zeke couldn't imagine. And in this world, neither would ever know Zeke's regret.

As he had done week after week in this hell hole of a jail, Zeke dwelled on these things, and more, as day broke through the two barred slits high in the walls left and right. Unshaven and unwashed, he sat in the corner beside his cot, aware of his reek even in the relative cool of the morning. He had made his peace with the Almighty, but he couldn't stand the thought of Vennie and Mistress Young bearing such scorn for him all the way to Judgment Day, when finally, they no longer would see through a glass, darkly.

Zeke heard a screech above, and when he looked, he saw a crack of daylight growing wider until he squinted at the glare through the three-foot square of the open hatch. He expected a rope to lower a little hardtack and jerky—standard fare, morning, noon, and night—but wood banged wood, and the ladder dropped from the sky.

A silhouette appeared, merging with the ladder's upper reaches, and when Zeke saw a flowing skirt wave in the wind and a figure begin to descend, he rose and went closer. He had never had a visitor other than Will and Smithson, and this one was more ungainly than even the heavyset attorney. She carefully searched for each succeeding rung below, and once there, she paused as if collecting herself before continuing down.

When she came within arm's reach, she spoke.

"Zeke, it's Jessie."

"Miss Jessie?" Zeke said in surprise. From the base of the ladder, he reached for her arm. "Sure 'nough be careful."

In the flooding light, he saw that she had reason to be. Will had related that Jessie was in a family way, but the bulge in her dress told him that the moment might come any day. Once down, she faced him, her breathing labored.

"How come you here, Miss Jessie? Sure ain't no good place."

"Will Brite's been seeing you regular. Didn't want you to feel forgot."

"Awful lonesome, this place. Do plenty of talkin', just me and Boss Man up in them clouds."

Jessie glanced up at the hatch, and when Zeke checked, he saw the deputy peering down as if eavesdropping.

"Let's you and me be gettin' ourselves yonder," said Zeke.

As they relocated to the corner, the ladder rasped upward behind them. When the hatch slammed shut, Jessie became a mere shadow in the nearer window's meager light.

"Let's be talkin' quiet," warned Zeke. "Jailer man bad about a-listenin' in when Mr. Smithson come. Least, you gets a little fresh air under ol' window. Sure sorry the smell so bad. That sun gets higher, even them dead cows down Devils way smells some better."

"Zeke," said Jessie, "Will Brite had to go away."

"Yes'm, doin' it for me, sure 'nough."

"For you?" Jessie seemed surprised.

"You don't know? Gone off down to—"

"Don't tell me," she interrupted. "I don't want to know where. That way, I can't let it slip."

"Slip, Miss Jessie?"

"They'd bring him back right here beside you if they catch him."

Zeke rubbed the back of his neck. "I guess I be wore down where I can't think good, but what Will done bad?"

"Marrying me. I didn't even know . . ."

Jessie had answered quickly, but now she hesitated. When she abruptly went unsteady on her feet, Zeke violated propriety again and took her arm.

"Sits you'self down on ol' cot here. Ain't been scratchin' with the lice or nothin'."

For a while, she sat quietly, her lowered brow in her hand. He was confused by her words, and by the way she had seemed to realize that she had said too much.

"How Will done bad marryin'?" he eventually asked.

He heard a weary sigh as her head rose.

"We . . . We're not hurting anybody, not *anybody*," she managed. "I—I don't . . . can't understand. Law . . . We came to find out they could lock him away, two years, maybe five, marrying somebody with colored blood."

Zeke hadn't known, either. He supposed there was a lot a colored man raised as a slave hadn't learned.

"You too, Miss Jessie? They throw you in ol' jail, family ways and all?"

She shook her head. "Sheriff says it's all on Will Brite. I . . . I don't know what I'm going to do, Zeke, him gone, my time coming quick."

Zeke turned away a moment, his burden so much greater than before. "Sure wish Will had gone and told me. Worryin' hisself to death over me when he got so much else to fret over."

"I guess he didn't want to make you feel any worse. I didn't mean to either. He keeps saying you've done more for him than any man there is."

"I sure be glad you told me, Miss Jessie. Now when I talk with Man on High, I puts in a good word for Will. You too."

"Zeke," she said, "You're awful kind, like . . . like . . ."

Zeke knew what she was unable to say. *Like Will Brite.*

"Sure wish I could help someways till he comes back," he said.

"He . . . He can't come back. Not ever."

Zeke supposed he hadn't been thinking straight. *They'd go and lock him away, and Miss Jessie be just as alone.* The little one would no more have a pappy than had the orphaned Zeke at age nine, and all because Jessie had been born to a life she hadn't chosen.

But there was more.

If Will had to stay on the run, there would never be a way to get Master Young's money to his suffering widow. She would go right on believing that Zeke had repaid his long years of kindness by killing him for a belt full of gold pieces, and she and sweet Vennie would celebrate when Zeke danced at rope's end before gasping women and gawking schoolchildren.

The troubling thought persisted as Zeke felt again the recoil of the forty-five that had changed lives forever. If only his finger hadn't slipped inside the trigger guard . . . If only the unintentional shot had found the corner post instead of Master Young . . .

If only, Vennie! If only!

"Zeke, how come . . ." Jessie broke the uncomfortable silence, but only at the price of a lot of emotion in her voice. "Zeke, how come life's so hard?"

"Some of us got it comin'. Almighty, He puts awful whippin' on me till I make it right with Him back at you' pappy Caleb's grave. Now, I be able to show my face come Judgin' Day."

"Is that what He's doing now? Punishing Will Brite and me for marrying?"

"Don't know that you gone and done wrong. Almighty, He tell us, sure will, so be a-listenin'. Me and Will, we talks about it a lot, big snow and all, if they be anything Boss Man can't wash away. Almighty big on forgivin', but He taken me through a awful lot till I find out."

Jessie stifled a sob. "Does . . . Does it get easier? Any easier at all?"

"If it be hard, 'member, Miss Jessie—this ain't our home. Just a-passin' through on way to glory land."

In a way, Zeke could hardly wait. But his regret about Vennie, and now about those gold pieces that Mistress Young would never see . . .

"You do somethin' for me?" he asked.

Jessie straightened. "What is it? You know I will." Then the emotion came again. "You—You're all I've got, now that Will Brite's . . ."

And she, in turn, was all Zeke had.

"Maybe you writes letters for this colored person?" he asked. "I sure be obliged."

CHAPTER 8

Even now, with Zeke in jail in faraway Vernon awaiting execution, twenty-year-old Vennie expected to see him riding in from Kansas with Andrew Young.

Day after day, as her servant duties allowed, she had climbed into the cupola atop the two-story Young plantation home near wooded Varners Creek in Brazoria County on the Texas Gulf Coast. From this roofed, eight-foot-square observatory with double windows on all sides, she had waited for a plume of dust to rise over the sugar mill and the sharecropper fields of cane.

Through two twelve-month growing seasons, and more, she had watched as field hands had grubbed, planted, irrigated, and hoed. Most troubling had been the day each fall when workers had torched the fields to strip the leaves so the sugar cane could be cut. Assuredly, the leaping flames and boiling smoke had reminded her of that awful place of fire and brimstone that, in her darker moments, she had found herself.

On this morning, she drew her focus back from the distance to her reflection in the windowpane. Zeke had always told her how pretty she was, but under the white dusting cap fitted about her black curls, she saw only a portrait of loneliness and despair in a high-collared dress of calico with a pattern of small diamonds.

She lifted her hand, her baggy sleeve clinging at the wrist, and traced her features in the glass: the smooth brown skin, the nose and lips more like some white ancestor than those of many field hands, the high forehead and dark eyes. But there was such sadness in those eyes . . . in the way her brow pinched . . . in the downward bend of the corners of her mouth.

Vennie was not only crushed, but lost. There had been no other way to think of herself since word had come that Master Young had died by Zeke's hand.

And now he would hang.

She heard a screech from behind, and she turned to see the hatch door rising from the plank flooring. A hand emerged, pushing the door back as a broad sleeve draped down a forearm.

"Vennie?" asked a gentle voice. "You up here?"

"Yes'm, I be here."

As Mistress Young appeared in the shadowy square that dropped into the attic, Vennie took her extended hand and helped her out. Once the hatch was secure again, the middle-aged woman, dressed in an ankle-length gray serge with a frilly white collar against her neck, stood against the backdrop of a high chimney. Beyond lay the greenery of gums, hickories, and shoe-peg maples, all interwoven with rattan and mustang grape vines. Towering above all were a few straight-trunked loblolly pines.

"Darling," said Mistress Young, "you been crying again, haven't you."

Vennie's emotions broke through so often that she was barely aware of them anymore. But only through a mist did she see the older woman: the kind brown eyes, the dainty chin, the mouth hesitant to smile and yet needing to. Sunlight highlighted the amber pins that Vennie herself had placed in the wavy hair bunched at back. When Master Young had ridden away, those locks had been dark, but now the white streaks shone, and wrinkles etched the corners of her eyes and scored her cheeks.

"I . . . I guess these windows have been stained with tears," Mistress Young added, not without difficulty. "Both of ours."

"It be hard, Mistress. It be awful hard."

"I know. It gets better for a spell, and then . . ."

"Zeke wouldn't ever did it. He just wouldn't've ever. Master Young like a pappy to him. Just like . . . Just like . . . you's a mama to me now."

Even though Vennie retained the dialect of her earliest years, she didn't like to remember her life before Mistress Young had taken her in from an overwhelmed sharecropper family. Now, mother-like, Mistress drew her close, and as Vennie laid her head on the woman's shoulder, the window wasn't the only thing moistened.

"Bless your heart." The older woman's voice choked a little. "But you've got more than me. The Good Lord's here. He's always here, never forgetting you."

Even inside Mistress's embrace, Vennie trembled. "But that be how I feels. Zeke, he gone. Master Young too. And now I be all alone, exceptin' for you's."

Drawing back a little, Vennie looked into eyes that glistened, much as her own must have.

"My poor, poor darling." The older woman smoothed her hand down Vennie's shoulder blade. "Don't give up hope. Not for Zeke. Not for the Good Lord."

"But Zeke gots no hope. They fixin' to hangs him."

"Wait on the Good Lord, Vennie. His justice is a lot stronger than the hangman's."

Mistress Young had spoken this way ever since news of Zeke's arrest had come. Vennie hadn't understood it then, and she didn't understand it now.

"You's awful kind. I don't sees how. Losin' Master Young, you's awful kind to me, way you's speaks 'bout Zeke."

The older woman began to blink a lot and she turned away, dabbing at her eyes.

"Mr. Young and me," she said, "losing our children young . . . I expect he felt the same way about Zeke that I do you. Till I know different about what happened, he deserves a chance."

"What chance a colored person gots, Mistress? Master Young be white, same as the judgin' men." Vennie glanced back across the fields and remembered what it was like to see dust billow from Zeke's approaching horse. "I . . . I won't never be seein' him come ridin' up. Not no more ever. Just like you never be seein' Master Young."

She thought she heard a sob. With Mistress Young's back to her, Vennie leaned close and, placing her cheek against the twilled fabric of the woman's dress, she shared the quake of the shoulder blades and prayed the way Mistress had taught her.

———

To Vennie, it seemed that Zeke walked at her side this morning, even though he was facing hanging in a faraway land.

For day after day, they had met here on Varners Creek, which divided the grounds of the two-story plantation home, with its white colonnade, from the sugar mill and sprawling fields of cane. Now, as then, cicadas buzzed from the sassafras saplings, while the stream gurgled, and a whisper of wind rustled the overhead greenery of shoe-peg maples and sycamores. When the climbing grapevines had been in season, Zeke had plucked grape after grape and placed them on her tongue. On his fingers, they had been as sweet as cane molasses, but never so sweet as his promises.

Vennie would never get over him. She didn't *want* to get over him. She would cling to the memories, for her life was as entwined with his as the hickories and gums were interwoven by rattan.

Deadfall snapped behind Vennie, and she turned to see Mistress Young approaching, a dogwood shrub tugging at the skirt of her dark serge.

"Thought you might be down here, Vennie," said the older woman, stopping before her. "Creek's kind of special to you, isn't it."

"Yes'm, it . . . it . . ." There was nothing else Vennie could say about the place where she and Zeke had dreamed of so many things.

"You poor thing. Didn't think you had tears left to cry." There was tension in Mistress's voice and in her raised eyebrows.

"Don't be worryin' 'bout me," whispered Vennie. "I—I be good."

But Vennie wasn't so sure of Mistress Young's welfare, for the older woman's shoulders bent and her chin fell against her frilly white collar.

"What be the matter, Mistress?"

The cicadas continued to hum as Mistress Young's pose stayed unchanged, and she looked up only after a deep sigh.

"As blue as you already are," said Mistress, "I don't know if seeing this will make things worse."

Reaching into her pocket, she brought out an envelope, prompting Vennie to crane for a better look.

A letter? Who be a-writin' a . . .

As the suspense grew along with her hope, Vennie didn't dare ask.

Mistress blew into the open envelope and parted it. "He addressed it to you," she said, withdrawing tally-book-sized pages. "So I didn't look at it."

Vennie quickly found her eyes. "*He*, Mistress Young?"

"Expect he had somebody write it for him. Get closer and we'll read it together."

Vennie's heart raced in a way that it hadn't since word had first come that Zeke had killed Master Young. She couldn't catch her breath, but that didn't keep her from pressing nearer so that she could see over the woman's shoulder. Abruptly, the smudged pencil script was only a blur, but as Mistress Young began reading aloud, Vennie seemed to hear it in dialect as if Zeke himself were speaking.

Please don't hate me, sweet Vennie. Please don't never.

Vennie sobbed and her knees wanted to buckle. As Zeke's voice persisted, she held to Mistress's arm.

Things gone right, we be married right now. We be home in new cabin Master Young built us. I be havin' ever'thing I ever wants—Master Young, best man I ever knowed, and Mistress Young, oh, how nice she been to this colored person. But mostest, I be havin' you.

Oh Vennie, they lookin' to hang this colored person, and I ain't never be seein' you no more. But come Judgin' Day, you finally be understanding what gone on that awful time when Master Young go slidin' down that post outside that poison joint. My hand be on that trigger, yes'm, so if they hangs me, I gets what's comin' to me. Just 'member they's more to it, no matter how bad they says of me.

Oh Vennie, sweet Vennie, of all the things this hard life done to this poor colored soul, I be the sorriest knowin' you hates me.

Now Vennie's legs did give way, and only a quick hand from the older woman kept her from collapsing.

"Oh Mistress, Mistress! I don't hates him! I don't, I don't!"

"I know it. I—I know it as well as you do." As she had in the cupola, Mistress Young wrapped Vennie in her arms. "Zeke wrote me too, wishing I . . . I wouldn't hate him either."

"You's got to hates him. Zeke's hand be on the gun, he say. How could Zeke did it, Mistress?"

For a moment, the older woman couldn't find words. "He says there's more to it—he wrote me that too," she eventually said. "Oh, if the Good Lord would just let us know for certain!"

Vennie shook in her embrace while grim shadows seemed to descend, smothering and choking all hope. Mistress must have felt it too, for Vennie noticed that she trembled with every emotional word that she added.

"Bless your heart, I—I know it hurts worse than anything. But listen—there's more he wrote."

Vennie couldn't have stood without support, and she kept her cheek against Mistress's bosom and looked on as the woman freed one hand and resumed reading. Again, Vennie heard the words as if Zeke himself spoke.

My friend Will Brite—he won't let me call him Mister Will—he done awful lot for me. His Miss Jessie—she sure in family ways—be real nice to me too. She the one writes this letter while Will gone off from jail town to help me. He say he fixin' to bring back the man caused Master Young's killin', but I figure I don't sees Will no more till glory land.

When she finished reading, Mistress Young stared down at the letter for so long that Vennie relived every tender moment with Zeke. The memories dominated even as the woman repeated what Zeke had said: *He say he fixin' to brings back the man caused Master Young's killin'.*

Vennie felt the rise of the woman's breast.

"I . . . I wasn't going to tell you this," said Mistress. "But you've a right to know. A telegram came too, and Zeke's appeal was denied."

"Denied, Mistress?" asked Vennie, not understanding.

"Hold tight to me, darling. You've got to hold tight and be strong. They're to hang him a week from Monday."

The world suddenly swam and everything went black, and the next thing Vennie knew, she was lying in the grass and Mistress was kneeling over her, blotting out the latticework of greenery against the sky. Vennie could feel the wetness as the woman dabbed her forehead with a kerchief she must have dipped in the stream.

"Trust in the Lord, Vennie," said the woman. "No matter what happens, we've got to trust in the Lord. Soon as you're able, let's go pack our things. We have a train to catch."

CHAPTER 9

Will had seen men buried, and the most troubling part had been watching the dirt spray down on a good man's face.

At noon on this day, that's how the alkali seemed: a shovelful here, a shovelful there, covering up all the good that had been. It kicked up from the flinty hoofs ahead, those of 984 bovines initially, so Ratcliff had tallied. Rising, it hung in the air, a cloud as hazy as a future without Jessie. Even as Will snugged the bandana about his face, the alkali still crawled down his throat, a reminder with every choking breath that life was a struggle.

As a new hand, Will had drawn the unpleasant duty of riding drag. Arch was there too, on his left, and Tommy, on Will's right, the three of them bringing up the slowest beeves. The animals were mere scarecrows that crept and stumbled, more likely to leave a trail of carcasses than ever reach next water at Howard's Well.

Will wondered if that would be his fate as well: another marker on skeleton plain.

The sun was a fiery wheel suspended almost overhead, and its rays set him squinting in a way he hadn't since the glare of 1884's big snow had first blinded and then tortured him for weeks. The air was stifling, especially in the wake of marching beeves. When thousands of cattle had milled during the big drift blizzard, the generated heat may have saved his life, but now it threatened to hasten his end before he accomplished his mission.

"I dare say," Arch said wearily, "this is certainly a land with the curse of thirst upon it."

"Never seen nothin' like it," agreed Will. He scanned the hills on either side; through the thick dust, the gray folds and limestone rimrock seemed like the walls of perdition through the smolder of brimstone. "Even the Devils valley has got its river."

"A River Styx, perhaps, laden with death, but this place must be shunned by even the minions of His Satanic Majesty."

Still, Will had no choice but to keep the small Appaloosa—his drive horse of morning—nodding along, its own hoofs churning the beaten trace.

Two days before, after Will had bloated himself on water at Pecan Springs, he had helped push the herd to within striking distance of so-called Pecos Canyon, the drainage pointing the way up out of the Devils valley and northwest for the Pecos River. Cattle had staggered and fallen one after another, and Will had dismounted and twisted their tails to get them to rise. The few with which he had succeeded had gone down again within yards, their nostrils flaring and tongues hanging out. A day later, Will had again encouraged suffering beeves to forge on—animals that couldn't know that next water lay a death march away. Now they were past dry Johnson's Run on the third day out, and as a Hereford collapsed in front of him and drove a horn into the ground, Will simply rode on, leaving the cow with its tongue lolling in the dirt.

Dodging the heaving flank brought Will closer to Arch, and he used the opportunity to address him quietly.

"Our man Rail's up that way, isn't he? Ridin' swing?"

Arch took his roan wider and checked. "All nine or more digits of him, a quarter-mile distant. I can distinguish the stocking-legged chestnut the gentleman known as Fat roped out for him this morning."

"How we goin' to do this, Arch? Way these drags are movin', rest of the herd will be headin' out in the mornin' about the time we's gettin' to the beddin' grounds. Meantime, the hangman might be on the train for Vernon right now."

Arch looked at him, hesitated, and lowered his head. "Will, I think you should prepare yourself."

"You mean for them hangin' him?"

"I fear it's almost certainly inevitable."

In conditions like these, with his face streaming and his parched throat burning, Will didn't like to hear that. He may have lost Jessie and their child forever, and the thought of being stripped of the only driving force he had left was almost enough to bring him down to the dust so bitter at his Appaloosa's forefeet.

"Zeke and me been in some fixes before," Will reminded himself out loud. "Couldn't got pulled out with a block and tackle, seemed like. But we didn't never give up and got through it somehow."

"Perseverance will indeed carry a man a long way."

"I can't go tryin' no less now. Besides, doin' ever'thing I can for him's all I got to hold on to, with Jessie . . ."

Abruptly, all Will could see was his own saddle horn, that and Jessie. For a while, the bellow of cattle and the grind of thousands of hoofs dominated.

"Will," Arch eventually said, "when I inquired of you on the Slash Fives, you remained silent about Jessie."

"Some . . . Some things is hard to talk about." Will looked up. "Jessie's the hardest."

Arch fell silent, and after a few paces of his roan, he turned the animal after a straying Hereford. Will watched, appreciating the fact that his friend had chosen not to press him about Jessie. When the cow was back with the drags, Will found a deep breath.

"I married her, Arch."

There was surprise in the uplift of Arch's eyebrows as he turned.

"I . . . I guess I shouldn't ought to have," Will added.

"I knew you were smitten by her—what a wondrous angel she is. But I had no inkling that the two of you had wed."

"Yeah," Will said quietly. "We was startin' a family. Hadn't been for Zeke's troubles, couldn't've been happier, neither one of us. Didn't know I done her wrong, marryin'. Still don't, I guess. All I know is I . . ."

Will's eyes began to burn and he turned away, not wanting Arch to see the emotion. "Don't know if I'll . . . I'll ever see her again."

He closed his eyes, shutting off a world in which he had found forgiveness for a boy's sins, only to grieve the Almighty, perhaps, in another way.

"Will," he heard Arch say, "I would never be so presumptuous as to consider myself an authority on matters of the heart. But there are times when everyone in a personal crisis needs the ear of a friend."

It wasn't a cowboy's way. It wasn't Will's way. But he brushed his eyes and looked at Arch.

"Just . . . Just not ready right now," Will managed.

He didn't think he would ever be ready.

As was typical of a drive, the drags ambled along in a column fifty or sixty feet wide, and as Will edged back to a center position, he heard Tommy mumble to himself. Tommy had done so ever since Pecan Springs, and the two things that he repeated most were "mean man" and "poor Mr. Wash." Will couldn't imagine what life was like for Tommy, and for somebody with his problems to be saddled with a matter so clearly troubling seemed another example of how unfair the world could be.

But in a moment of darkness in which Will yearned for Jessie's touch, he remembered how she had said that God's hand is stronger than anything that life can throw at a person. Maybe Tommy just needed a friend who had learned that firsthand.

"Tommy," he said, "you've been off your feed ever since Pecan Springs. Why don't you ride on up to the wagon and grab a bite. Get your water ration while you're at it."

Tommy turned. "I better be a-stayin'. Mr. Wash say, 'You bring 'em on, Tommy. You bring 'em, one ol' cow at a time.'"

"He didn't mean for you not to eat."

"Can't let Mr. Wash down no more. Poor Mr. Wash, he—"

"Tell you what," interrupted Will. "I'll go with you. I'm gettin' pretty weak at the craw." He turned to Arch for a moment. "You hold down the fort for a little bit? Me and Tommy's goin' for chuck."

"I shall indeed man the parapets."

Will veered right and took the Appaloosa around the hindquarters of the redhead's bay. Rather than press the young cowhand, Will simply said, "Come on, Tommy," and started up the side of the herd. Sometimes a person responded better if something was expected of him.

Surely enough, the rattle of a saddle from behind told Will that Tommy followed. After a few strides, Will slowed and let him come abreast on his left. Loping their horses, the two of them advanced steadily on point.

Tommy began muttering again, something about his fear of riding upon a fresh grave marked by an upright wagon plank inscribed *Wash Baker, shot in back.*

"Tommy, you got to quit worryin' so much. My Jessie read me where . . ." Only after lowering his head a moment could Will go on. "Good Lord says don't go frettin' about tomorrow. Today's got enough to deal with."

"Can't help it. My mama fretted all time. She left me on a doorstep, just a young'n I was, but ever'body talked about her, 'bout my pappy bein' same way. He was my uncle too, you know, uncle and pappy both, sure 'nough."

It took several seconds for Tommy's words to sink in, and when they did, Will was convicted in a way he hadn't been since the events of the big drift had repeatedly raised reminders of his sins as a ten-year-old.

Unnatural!

He and Tommy had overtaken the stronger cattle, and as Will studied the beeves through the V formed by Tommy upright in the saddle and the angling head of his bay, he saw that they were all cattalos.

The humps . . . the shaggy coats . . . the muscular hindquarters unlike any Hereford that had ever marched up a trail . . .

Back in '84 and '85, Will had been forced to face his inner hell through first Zeke and then Jessie, and now demons of a different breed seemed intent on never letting him forget the consequences of violating boundaries that the Almighty had put in place.

Abruptly, he didn't want to have anything to do with Tommy. Maybe Will should have felt as unclean as he had when a Black man—Zeke—had rescued him from under a thousand pounds of horse tangled in barbed wire as the blizzard of '84 had struck. But this was worse, for Will couldn't admit to himself, much less to the Almighty, that he and Jessie had done wrong.

Even so, he reeled with another memory of the circuit-riding preacher. From an Arbuckle Coffee crate, the man had recounted the words of the Good Lord when someone had resisted His call to make things right.

It's hard for you to kick against the goads.

With a long goad rod, Will had separated enough cattle through the slats of railroad cars to understand. And then, a few strides after he and Tommy passed Fat on point, Tommy complicated matters more.

"Awful good, Will, you bein' my friend. Mr. Wash, he my friend too, like Miss Emma and their little miss. But you's the only friend I got these parts."

Even when the big drift blizzard had howled out of the north and the mere sight of a colored man had tormented Will with images of a Texarkana slave cabin in flames, Will had found it within himself to bring Zeke inside the Slash Five line shack, despite the protests of Wampus. Now Will was tested again, and he didn't know if he had the courage to do the right thing.

His immediate response was to look out over his Appaloosa's ears and dwell on things. Rocking in the saddle, he was only vaguely aware of the wagon bows rising against the dusty horizon ahead, and of the smoke drifting from a cook fire. The herd and remuda had moved out at first light, leaving the *cocinero* to break camp, but the chuck wagon had soon rumbled by on the way to the spot where the cattle were expected by midday. There, meals and fresh horses would await cowhands when they arrived in shifts.

Guarding against throwing a dust, Will secured his horse to a scrub mesquite well shy of the wagon and proceeded on foot. Close on his left, his gait as gangly as ever, walked Tommy, still going on about his friends Mr. Wash, Miss Emma, Little Miss—and Will. As their spurs jingled, Tommy asked him a question, and asked it again, but Will stayed silent until a rider came up from behind, the rhythm of the hoofbeats indicating a lope.

"Get your butt back on drag, Clabberhead."

Will looked in time to see Rail's horse surge past Tommy so closely that had the redhead taken a step to the left, the stocking-legged chestnut would have struck him. Startled, Tommy dodged, and so did Will.

"What's the cla—?" Will nearly said *clabberhead*. "What's he up to?" He recognized Rail, who maintained a lope even as the dust followed him toward the wagon. "He almost run us over."

"That Rail, he thinks he a mean'n," said Tommy. "He ain't never seen mean for hisself likin' I seen. They's mean, and they's *mean*."

Will watched Rail lope his horse right up to the weathered side-board of the wagon before drawing rein.

"He's sure goin' to catch it from the *cocinero*," said Will. "They call him Hub, don't they?"

Fanning the blowing dust, the aging cook burst around the chuck box on the right, the catch in his stride a sign of the stove-up old cowboy he probably was. Behind the scraggly gray facial hair, and especially in the knotted eyebrows, was plenty of fight, but after Hub's mouth flew open as if ready to deliver a tongue-lashing, he wiped his hands on his greasy apron and spat out his quid. As tobacco juice dribbled down his jaw, he tugged on his goatee and looked on in silence as Rail dismounted.

When Rail tied the chestnut to the front wheel, he violated a second unwritten rule of a wagon camp, but Hub only worked his toothless gums and stared.

"Never saw a cook worth his salt let somebody get away with that," said Will.

"That Rail, he got near' ever'body buffaloed 'cept Mr. Ratcliff," said Tommy. "But he don't know what Tommy seen. I seen what mean is."

By this time, Will was close enough to see the leak from the metal-banded water barrel secured against the sideboard. A cast iron pot was on the ground below, catching the steady drip-drip. The pot was nearly full, and at the rate that new concentric circles formed in the glassy surface, it was clear that a lot of water had been lost when the wagon had been on the move.

Rail came around the chestnut's hindquarters and Hub met him at the barrel. When the cook removed the lid, the cowhand grabbed a ladle from a nail in the sideboard and dipped it into the water. Will winced as Rail brought it dripping to his lips, for it reminded him of how flushed Jessie had been when he had ridden back from the jail and fetched her a drink.

That last afternoon with her, and the night and daybreak that had followed, would live inside him forever.

Rail turned the dipper bottom up, draining the last drop, and then plunged it into the barrel again.

"Ratcliff says . . . says one dipper a man," Hub said timidly.

Rail brought up another streaming ladle full and looked at him. "I don't expect you gonna be sayin' nothin' to him, are you." It was a statement made in such a way not to be questioned. He glanced at Tommy approaching at Will's side. "Clabberhead there don't do nothin' to get thirsty. I'm drinkin' his."

Will knew that Tommy would react, and he did.

"I need me a drink bad!" he told Will. "Ol' throat dry and he say—"

"I know what he said, Tommy," interrupted Will, drawing Rail's attention. They were within a few steps of Rail now. "But he don't rule the roost around here."

In obvious challenge, Rail brought the dipper to his lips, his dark eyes mere slits above it as they fixed on Will. For an extended moment, the glare persisted, and then Rail gulped the water so thoughtlessly that much of it ran down the sides of his mouth.

Zeke was going to hang in place of maybe a man like this.

This time, the thought was even more powerful than before, and as Rail returned the ladle to its nail and stepped toward Will—perhaps intent only on circling around the chestnut—Will stopped and looked back at the Appaloosa and the burlap sack that concealed the Schofield.

Spur rowels jangled oddly, and then came Tommy's startled cry and a violent thud like a calf flanked at a branding fire. Spinning, Will saw the redhead sprawl to the ground before the barrel, his flailing arm turning the cast iron pot on its side.

"Water a-spillin'!" exclaimed Hub.

As the *cocinero* lunged under the barrel to save what he could, Rail stood looking down through the stirring dust at Tommy. "Knocked the damned pot over!" he yelled.

"Didn't mean to! Didn't mean to!"

"Clumsy as you is dumb!" Rail added.

"Didn't mean to! Didn't mean to!"

Was that the hint of a self-satisfied smile on Rail's lips again?

Tommy, rolling to his hip under the barrel, was a forlorn figure behind the drip as he faced Will. "Didn't mean to, Will! Don't go not bein' my friend no more!"

Will didn't know how to respond, especially with so much distress in the young man's face. All he knew was that Tommy's need for his friendship was one more thing that seemed determined to take Will's measure as a man.

"Trip over your own feet?" Will managed.

"That and more, I reckon," muttered Hub, positioning the pot under the drip again.

When the cook gave a furtive look at Rail, and Rail looked back, Will knew there was more to Tommy's fall than a stumble. Could the cowhand that Will suspected of so much have been so childish—and cruel—as to have extended his boot and tripped Tommy? Wouldn't it have been that sort of man who would have pistol-whipped Zeke outside the tavern and caused Andrew Young's death? This very moment, a hangman might be fitting Zeke, not Rail, for a noose! The SOB, what was he hiding in the stiff ring finger of that glove?

Will started toward him, hellbent on seizing his hand—but suddenly a shout from behind punctuated the rising drum of hoofs.

"Everybody to the herd! Duster coming!"

Will turned on his heel and saw Ratcliff riding up, his sorrel horse raising its own alkali storm. The boss pointed to the north, and over the nervous horses in the bunched remuda, Will saw a wall of dirt over the irregular hills of the nearby horizon. Black as coal, it rose higher by the second, a ring-tailed terror with towering pillars turning end over end.

"It's the end of the world!" yelled Hub.

Abruptly Tommy was at Will's side. "Will . . . Will . . . He say . . . !"

As the tumbling columns bore down on Will with frightening speed, he saw plenty in the ever-changing clouds: a face, maybe, or multiple faces, that of the Almighty in judgment, or the devil in hell waiting to receive the unrepentant who had crossed boundaries not to be tested. Then another shout shook him into action.

"Let's get to our cows, boys!" ordered Ratcliff.

A step ahead of Tommy, Will ran for the Appaloosa. They had hitched their horses only loosely to the mesquite chaparral, and the skittish animals were trying to break free, the reins yanking the limber branches. Just in time, Will arrived and seized the Appaloosa by the cheek of the bridle. Thorns ripped his hand as he freed the reins, but at least he had control of his horse, while Tommy's bay pulled free and trotted away.

"He done gone!" exclaimed Tommy. "My horse, Will, he done gone!"

With the booger that was barreling out of the north, Will couldn't imagine leaving a man afoot, especially Tommy, and as soon as he mounted up, he gigged the Appaloosa after the runaway. He quickly overtook the horse, but the terrified bay almost escaped his hold before Tommy ran up and swung astride.

Reining the Appaloosa for the herd, Will glanced back. In the brief time since Ratcliff had given warning, the clouds had swept halfway up the sky, a black bruise blazed under the blue.

"Keep your hat over your eyes!" yelled Will. "Tie it down or you'll lose it!"

Will untied a saddle string and passed it across the crown of his hat. It wasn't easy, securing it under his chin as he galloped his horse for the cattle, but he had a loose knot in place when he checked over his shoulder again. Past Tommy, whose crooked mouth was agape as he fumbled with his own knot, the wagon was dwarfed by the boiling clouds. High in the sky, almost overhead, ghostly streamers led the way.

It was a storm that could make ghosts, too, of men and animals, and as Will looked ahead, he saw cowhands frantically trying to tighten the herd. But a drove that stretched half a mile was impossible to bunch in mere moments, and just as the Appaloosa reached the cattle, an incredible wind almost blew Will out of the saddle.

Something else happened as well.

The sun went out.

CHAPTER 10

If Will hadn't seen the sandstorm coming, he would have thought he had gone blind.

But he could feel plenty: the sting of grit as powerful as constant blasts from a twelve-gauge shotgun with salt-loaded shells. He couldn't breathe, not even when he buried his face alongside the Appaloosa's neck. The long mane whipped his hat and muffled every sound, but there was no denying the wind's roar.

A phantom bumped Will's leg, and bumped it again, jostling the Appaloosa. Then something hard and sharp raked his thigh and he seemed caught up in an unstoppable current bearing with the wind. Horns clacked all around, a drumbeat in the bellowing of cattle, and he knew that he was trapped in a violent surge of animals instinctively fleeing a storm.

Will remembered another duster, at Beaver Lake on the Devils, where he had helped carry a half-drowned Arch to the shelter of a cabin. That storm had brought into his life a young nester woman who had proved a shining light brighter than any sun dimmed by an ordinary sandstorm. But this was the kind of black blizzard that disoriented and crushed hope in a man's soul, and all Will could do was give the Appaloosa its head and accept whatever was meant to happen.

Maybe it would be a horse wreck that would throw him under the trampling hoofs. Maybe it would be worthy punishment for a man forgiven once, only to backslide and commit another sin as grievous in its own way. He called upon the Almighty to help him, but why should a righteous God render aid to someone who wouldn't—who *couldn't*—confess that he had done wrong and beg forgiveness?

He loved Jessie! He would always love her and treasure their every moment together even if cast into torments!

In a darkness greater in every way than any he had known, Will had never felt so alone. "You there, Tommy?" he shouted. "Tommy! You there?"

But Will couldn't hear his own voice, not even when he yelled again, and as he clung to the Appaloosa, he was terrified by the thought that death was upon him and he was being swept away into perdition's deepest corner. And yet his love for Jessie stayed strong, an emerging spark of hope against a night without end.

For minutes or hours, he held fast to Jessie's love as the Appaloosa carried him on. Then a light flashed—or had he imagined it?—and when Will turned his head to his horse's flank, he saw momentary discharges outlining clashing horns. A fire there and yet not there, it was at once blue-green, reddish-yellow, and misty purple, a horde of imps riding the sea of horns.

He had seen lightning dance on a herd before, at a time when jagged sky-fire had split the night and thunder had blared. But this was different—unholy—and his fear grew until he remembered Arch telling of such a phenomenon in a nighttime sandstorm on the buffalo range. The air had become so charged, Arch had explained, that not only had the iron wagon tires burned with eerie flames, but they had delivered a jolt to the touch.

The explanation was beyond Will's understanding, but whether natural or devilish, the display was no less unnerving.

Conditions ultimately grew almost imperceptibly brighter, and when he checked, he found a glowing wheel low in the sky. It vanished and reappeared, a fleeting promise that the sun still burned somewhere beyond the swirling wraiths bent on destroying. For only moments the dim orb showed itself before the dark swallowed it so completely that Will wondered if it had ever been there.

About that time, horns hooked his legs from both sides and his pony rocked in a different way to unseen forces. No longer was the relentless wind squarely at Will's back, but it punished him from ever-changing angles. When it struck broadside and finally head on, he recognized the curving course that had seized the Appaloosa.

Will had been here before. He had *lived* this before, in a blinding whiteout in the big drift blizzard when a herd had caught him up on the divide between the Middle Concho and Devils rivers. It was an eddy of muscled beeves and irrepressible horns, an instinctive mill in extreme weather. Before, it had served to generate heat and shield against flesh-peeling wind, for tightly packed beeves in perpetual motion would spiral in on themselves. This time, with the heat already unbearable, the cattle must have been forced into a mill by a geographic feature—a deep gully, perhaps, or a rocky battlement—that blocked their retreat from the wind.

As dangerous as flight had been, this frenzy of bruising swipes and sparring horns was worse, and just as in '84, Will rode in dread of a gouging horn that could spill the Appaloosa's entrails and bring him down with his mount. It wouldn't have required *that* much, for if a beef collapsed in his horse's path, the end would be the same.

A mill's driving current funneled animals inside and then outside in a never-ending cycle, and Will could gauge his location by the direction and force of the wind and the difference in temperature. Once, twice, three times he reached the outer streamer, his horse fading more and more. The fourth time, he took a chance while there was still hope, and cut the Appaloosa sharply left in front of a pair of glowing horns.

Bumped hard, the Appaloosa remained upright, but there was another spiral arm to breach, and another. Will didn't know how his horse managed to keep its balance, but suddenly the two of them were free.

"Hyaah!"

Opening the Appaloosa up into a faltering gallop, Will rode into the teeth of the storm. He had to distance himself from the cattle, but his mount was all but spent. He could feel its heart pounding against his leg, and he weighed the danger of the mill against being set afoot in a half-acre of hell if he rode the animal to death.

He had just eased the horse into a lope when the Appaloosa went down, and momentum drove him over its head.

———

Will's eyes were open, but he was asleep, and Jessie darted in and out of dreams that seemed more than dreams.

She was in the night, calling his name, smoothing fingers across his brow, but she was back on the Pease as well, her face flushed as he turned to the water bucket in the pecans. He had to get her a drink and ease the fire that he could strangely see in her throat, but his legs were leaden, unable to move no matter how hard he tried.

Jessie! Jessie!

He tried to call her name, but his voice wouldn't work, not even as she pleaded with him.

Water . . . Get me water . . . water . . .

The hoarse word, as powerful as any Will had ever known, came with him out of his fog, and when the night showed itself all around, he realized that he heard his own voice.

"Water . . . water . . ."

The plea crawled up out of a throat that burned as if lodged with a hot coal, and as he passed a hand across his forehead where Jessie had seemed to caress, he felt a decided knot. His other hand was clenched, but something tugged on it, and several seconds elapsed before he understood that he sprawled under his horse's stirring hoofs, the reins still firmly in his control.

The black blizzard had passed, but dust must have hung in the air, for overhead he saw stars through a haze. He could taste the dirt, and he seemed to have difficulty breathing. But worst of all was his thirst, dehydration so intense that his tongue clung to his palate. The storm had denied him a drink at the wagon, and he couldn't make spittle, not even to expectorate the grit between his teeth.

He sat up, a little dizzy, and pulled the Appaloosa closer with the reins. He found the stirrup leather and dragged himself to his feet. Unsteady, he held to the saddle and shook his head, trying to clear his senses fully. Listening, he could no longer hear the pound of hoofs in a mill, only the *yip* of coyotes in the distance. They were oddly comforting, for their song told him that this was someplace other than perdition, no matter what he might have done to deserve that fate.

Still, the loneliness was immense, loneliness for Jessie, for another voice, for anything to reassure him that he wasn't the only one to survive the end of the world.

If only it was daylight. . . . If only there was something to buoy his spirits in this depressing dark . . .

From alongside the tobacco tin in his linsey-woolsey shirt, he drew a match and struck it on the saddle. The tiny flame served only to make his surroundings blacker and more vexing, and he looked about for wood with which to build a fire. Leading the Appaloosa, he exhausted several more matches before he came upon a rat's nest under a catclaw bush.

As he tied the horse to a scrub mesquite on the left and approached the haphazard pile of twigs, memory cautioned him to watch for rattlesnakes. He had lived this too before, in the big drift blizzard after eluding another mill, and he marveled at the forces that again set the stage for self-examination of how he may have grieved the Almighty.

In '84, when he had stoked the fire by which Zeke had saved his life a second time, a devil-eyed rattler had hung its fangs in Will's leggings, a taste of the punishment due him for sins as a boy. Absolved once, could he hope to escape judgment twice?

Now, twenty months later, Will found a three-foot limb under his horse's forelegs and used it to rake the twigs out into the open. By feel, he built a tiny tepee around bunched grass. A coating of dust was a hindrance, and he exhausted the matches in his pocket and had to get more from his war bag, but finally he had a fledgling fire going.

Mere light improved his outlook, even in circumstances so grim— and then came a stark reminder of boundaries not to be breached.

"Will? Will? Please be Will! Please, please!"

Even if he hadn't seen the gangly silhouette approaching from the left and leading a horse, Will would have recognized the panicky voice. Moments ago, Will had longed for even a manifestation of natural law profaned, as Arch may have put it, but the fire had eased his concerns. Nevertheless, when Tommy called again, Will steeled himself and did the right thing.

"Tie your horse yonder by mine," he said.

Even at a distance, Will could hear a sob.

"He . . . He say it the end of the world! Hub, he say—"

"You and me's still here, anyway. A lot of those cattle too, I expect."

"They—They taken the stompede devils. I—I whispered in ol' horse's ear, 'You be all right, all right, sure 'nough. But horns pokin' him all time, us a-runnin' right in the middle of 'em. I scared like nobody's business, but I couldn't let on to ol' bay, no sir."

"You got a way with horses," Will said truthfully. *About as good as anybody I ever saw.*

"I get him unsaddled now, brush him down with bunched grass. Ol' Appaloosy too, if you want me to."

Will didn't want Tommy's help. He didn't want anything to do with him, not someone who so convicted him of how he may have wronged Jessie. But off to the right, a dead mesquite stood in the flickering light, and he needed to gather its ample fuel before the fire went out.

"Horses need takin' care of, all right," he said quietly. "Go ahead." He wanted to add, *Be obliged to you*, but couldn't bring himself to.

With the horses addressed and staked, Will sat before the fire. He could see residual dust floating in the firelight, and he didn't know which was the better representation of the Almighty's judgment: the black blizzard or the hissing flames lapping wood that groaned as if in pain. Either way, it wasn't a pretty picture, and he found himself resenting Tommy in a way he once had taken exception to Zeke.

"Somebody send you?" he asked. Tommy sat on his left, but Will's gaze stayed on the fire.

"Mr. Wash, he tells me, 'You bring 'em on, Tommy. Rest of them cattle, you bring 'em. That ol' Pecos, I be there waitin' on you.'"

"More to it than that, I figure."

"Huh?"

An agent of judgment should have understood, but maybe Tommy's role was to force Will to face up to a sin entirely different from what he had committed when a long-ago fire had roared in the Texarkana night. Abruptly, he remembered something else that the roundup preacher had related: how King David not only had committed adultery with Bathsheba but had arranged to have her husband killed in battle to hide the fact that it was David's son she carried. David had crossed not only one line but two, and part of his penalty had been the pain he had suffered when the infant had died.

Would any judgment that Will might incur also sweep up the baby whom Jessie might give birth to at any time? Even if spared, would their child carry a mark of boundaries violated, as did Tommy?

"What ... What's it like?" As Will spoke, he studied Tommy in the fire glow: the twisted mouth, the crooked teeth, the crossed eyes that would never hold the smarts of a normal person. "Bein' like you are, what's it like?"

"Mr. Wash sure look out for me since I was a young'n. 'It's time, Tommy,' he tells me. 'You done rid with me on a drive to Kansas, so's I know you can do it good as anybody. You bring 'em, Tommy. I be waitin' on the Pecos for you.'"

Suddenly Tommy's shoulders slouched, and all energy drained from his face. "Poor Mr. Wash. That mean man. Poor Mr. Wash."

Not again, thought Will.

"Your mother and uncle—father, I guess," he said out loud. "You hold it against them?"

"Mama give me away, sure 'nough. Never knowed my mama or pappy either, just what they say about them. Ever'body mean to me till I was a big ol' kid and Mr. Wash taken me in. Poor Mr. Wash, I sure let him down. That mean man . . ."

As Tommy stared into the fire and continued, it was clear that he was incapable of the insightful discussion Will wanted. But the young man showed again that, in his own way, he was as troubled as Will.

"Tell him, Tommy," the redhead said to himself. "Tell Mr. Wash 'bout mean man. Tell him 'fore they go off together, headin' for the Pecos. Tell him what you seen on the Big Red."

The Big Red.

For a moment, Will was back on the boardwalk outside the tavern at Doans near the Red River point where countless cowhands had crossed herds in the push north. Zeke's problems had begun there, but Jessie believed it had all been part of the Almighty's plan to set him fleeing straight into Will's life. The two of them—Zeke and Jessie—had given Will someone to whom he could say he was sorry for what his ten-year-old self had done to their people.

"I gonna find it," Tommy went on. "I gonna find grave sayin' *Wash Baker, shot in back*, and it be my doin', all my doin'."

Tommy looked up, and Will had never seen a face so distraught.

"Think on it for me, Will," Tommy pleaded. "Do I got the bad place comin' when they buries me?"

It was the same issue Will had grappled with for years, until he had found peace after trying to charge his horse into a range fire in penance. Now he faced uncertainty again, and every moment around this person born so unnaturally made it worse. But Will couldn't just get on his horse and ride away, no matter how much he might wish to.

"Friend of mine, name of Zeke . . ." Will could barely hear himself through the alkali in his throat. He tried to cough it out but couldn't. "Anyway, he used to say the Good Lord's big on forgivin'. Guess I found it out for myself. Now, though . . ."

The swirling smoke blew into his face, burning his sinuses and stinging his eyes. It almost seemed a sign, and when he looked away, hacking worse, the smoke must have found Tommy.

"Can't stand it! Can't stand it! Can't stand it!"

"Just get up and move," said Will.

When Will checked, the redhead had already stepped away, but the smoke seemed bent on following him as he stumbled clockwise around the fire.

"It chasin' me! Ever' step, like Almighty chasin' me for not sayin' nothin'. Seen bad things twice and I too scared to say nothin'!"

Tommy kicked through the woodpile on Will's right and sprawled, and the moment he tried to rise, the smoke smothered him again.

"Stay down where it can't find you," said Will.

Or maybe the smoke was like judgment finding a person, no matter how hard he tried to hide his face. Zeke had talked about that very thing, and now Tommy obsessed about it too.

"Almighty got hold of me! Thirsty, awful thirsty! Mouth dry and throat burnin' up! What do I do, Will? What I got to do?"

Will couldn't answer the question even for himself. His lips were cracked, and he couldn't moisten them. His parched tongue seemed too thick to speak in more than a mumble, and every breath aggravated a throat already seared. His dehydration was bad enough at night, when the ground radiated the heat absorbed during the day. But in a few hours would come the sun, a window into hell that would burn with a deadly fury.

Maybe Will would get what he deserved. If so, he just prayed that Jessie and their baby wouldn't be caught up in his punishment.

CHAPTER 11

It's under your pillow, Jessie.

Jessie, it's under your pillow.

Jessie awoke to Will's voice from the cot an arm's length from hers. She lay facing it, and the words came so clearly that she gave a little gasp. Opening her eyes, she stretched out her hand, brushing the tin-banded chests stacked at the head of the cots, but there was nothing next to her except empty ducking drawn over a wooden frame. Beyond, between the support poles of the shelter, she could see the green-leafed pecans trembling in a breeze down by the Pease.

There seemed to have been another voice that had preceded Will's, and now, from behind, she heard it again: a surly voice with a backwoods twang that she had hoped never to hear again.

"Said, get yourself up, Little Pickaninny."

Jessie started, the cot screeching beneath her as she tried to turn. For weeks, she had been unable to roll over without Will's help, her abdomen too much a hindrance, and all she could manage was a glimpse over her shoulder of an unkempt form in the early morning light.

"What do you want?" she blurted in alarm.

"You's goin' with me," added the voice she recognized as Federson's.

She knew better than to turn her back on a rabid dog or Federson, but she had no choice in order to rise. Slipping her lower legs off the side of the cot, she got one hand under her on the ducking and the other on the frame and pushed herself up to a sitting position. Before she could stand, Federson blocked the narrow path between the cots.

"You's mine, case you forgot," he said, picking his bulbous nose. "Bought and paid for."

Federson was a wretch of a man, and he looked the part. If he had ever bathed since he had counted out money to her supposed father, Caleb, and wagoned her away six years ago, she couldn't have told it by his dreadful body odor. From his matted gray hair and tangled beard to his dingy woolen shirt and greasy duck trousers, he was repugnant, and when he showed his broken teeth, black with decay, it was clear that he had never learned to brush with a frayed root.

Federson wiped the mucus from his finger on his trousers and motioned to the chests with the same unsanitary hand.

"Get them things of yours together," he ordered.

Will Brite! Will Brite!

Jessie twisted about, silently calling, but Will wasn't there, and might never be again.

"No use lookin' for him," said Federson. "Hear he run out on you." Turning away a moment, he pressed the side of his nose and blew mucus out of the opposite nostril.

"Your doing," Jessie charged. "You started the talk, out of plain meanness."

"If you hadn't gone off from me like you done, back there when you was fifteen, wouldn't've been no call for it. Left me high and dry, you and Caleb both. Felt awful funny, me out all them dollars and come to find out you'd run back home and Caleb had took you off somewhere."

Somewhere, all right, eventually to the Devils River, but even if it had been all the way to Kingdom Come, it wouldn't have been far enough away from Federson and his lewd advances.

He continued. "Imagine me runnin' into you all the way out here outside that store, hearin' Caleb died and went to hell. Wouldn't be no collectin' from him, no sir. And that man you was with, husband, he sure wasn't goin' to let me take what was mine. I had ever' right to tell ever'body what I knowed about Little Pickaninny."

"You . . . You don't know *anything* about me," Jessie said unconvincingly.

"Oh, I know plenty. I can still see that colored man—free, they say, wasn't no slave—kickin' and hangin' from that big hickory once we tracked him down back in '63. Peddler, he was, sellin' venison and such out of a old wagon. Got a little too friendly with your mama, comin' around like he done. Guess she liked black stuff better than Caleb."

Jessie had never known her mother, but she would never be able to rid herself of memories of Caleb. A cruel, abusive drunkard, he had beaten Jessie unmercifully, and had he lived, he would have denied her a life of her own choosing. With a domineering husband like him to make every moment at home a hell on earth, Jessie couldn't fault her mother for finding someone gentle and caring.

"Nigger raped your mama, Caleb told ever'body," Federson went on. He had found more mucus to dig out of his nose. "Guess I was the only one he let on to 'bout the whorin' she done. Ol' tongue of his would get mighty loose if he spent enough time lookin' in a bottle."

He twisted his finger inside his nostril before continuing. "Oughta been there to seen your real pappy. Tied him to that hickory, standin' up there huggin' it. Ripped his shirt off of his back and Caleb goes to horse-whippin' him, the blood runnin' red against that black skin of his. Wasn't much left of him, time we got him swingin' from that tree, but won't never forget them white eyes bulgin' out and him a-messin' in his britches."

Graphic elements that Caleb had never revealed to Jessie, they burned into her mind a terrible picture of inhumanity and racial injustice. Her poor mama! Her poor mama! Jessie could just imagine her anguish when Caleb had delighted in telling her every last detail, and even though Caleb had been dead for more than fifteen months, Jessie hated him even more.

Federson, though, was very much alive, and because he had known the truth and still had participated, his guilt was just as great.

He reached for Jessie's arm, but she recoiled from his touch.

"Oh, you's goin' to get used it," he said. "Startin' tonight, you's goin' get used to me a-touchin' you."

"Go away!" she cried. "I—I've got a husband."

"Not no more, you ain't."

Federson seized her forearm, but Jessie wrenched free and again called silently for someone who had held her so tenderly their last night together.

Federson's face went dark. "Little hellcat, ain't you? No use you givin' me trouble this away. You ain't never bein' with that husband of yours again. Law won't allow it. Grand jury done indicted him."

Federson must have read the sheer hatred in her face, for his tone softened. "Tell you what, Little Pickaninny. They ever catch him and it goes to trial, they'll be callin' me in to testify. You come be with me from now on, promise you ain't runnin' off, and I'll forget what I know when I get in that witness chair. 'A white man's her papa, know that for a fact,' I'll tell them. 'Mama was white too,' I'll say. 'I was just spreadin' big windies 'round Vernon.'"

If it had been a matter of sacrificing her own future to ensure that Will would never face prison, Jessie might have gone with him. But there was another life to consider, one that kicked inside her this very moment—a gift from God she could never subject to someone like Federson.

"My . . . My baby's coming any day," she said, placing a hand on her abdomen. But was Federson even capable of caring?

His bloodshot eyes dropped, and he evidently studied her condition. "Ain't what I was figurin' on, another pickaninny around. But I can fix that. Soon as it's borned, I'll swing it by the heels up against the wagon wheel."

My baby!

Federson clutched her again, and the voice from her dream spoke more loudly than ever.

It's under your pillow, Jessie.

Jessie, it's under your pillow.

Federson had a vise grip above her right elbow, denying her use of her dominant arm. But that didn't keep her free hand from sliding under the pillow. She came out with cold steel, heavy and unnatural in her grip, but not so awkward that she couldn't thumb back the hammer. Suddenly she saw Federson's wide eyes down the revolver's seven-inch barrel.

"Pull a gun on me, will ya? I'll see to it he rots in prison."

"Go away! Go away!"

"Hell, you ain't shootin' *nobody*," he growled, and he lunged for the Colt.

For their baby, the only part of Will she might ever have again, Jessie would give up everything she was or hoped to be. She squeezed the trigger, and a roar shook the Pease bottom land where she and the gentlest of men had made a home all too briefly.

———————

Death stared him in the face.

It was in the sun, a fireball flaring on the eastern horizon. It was in the land, a desolate sea of mesquite chaparral stripped of foliage by the big blow. It was in the heat waves that set the barren hills shimmering, and in the rippled drifts of dust, caught on the windward side of occasional Spanish daggers.

But worst of all, death had crept into Will's mind, denying hope and convicting him that this was his judgment for wronging Jessie.

In the dismal gray of dawn, he and Tommy had spotted a faint plume of smoke in the northwest and started toward it, a powder rising from their horses' hoofs. As the wind had shifted, the haze had enveloped Will and heightened a headache that had raged with every struggling breath in the storm. With the sun beating down on his shoulders, he hadn't known how much more he could endure. But just as in the big drift blizzard, he had almost welcomed the misery, realizing by its very degree that he deserved whatever punishment the Almighty meted out.

Now, as he neared Hub's summoning fire, he lifted penitent eyes to the cloudless sky. *My doin', my fault! Do what you got to to me, but please, not to Jessie!*

But he feared that his transgression had swept her up as well, and their baby too, and his eyes burned for a reason that had nothing to do with the grit and glare of a land that didn't care. It didn't care that he might never be with Jessie again, or that Zeke was about to hang. When he and Tommy drew rein at the wagon camp, it was clear that the land cared even less that the roaring wind had lifted the wagon and slammed it on its side, for the mishap threatened the precious water barrel underneath.

The Bar X drovers were already there, several of them working to right the wagon by rope and horsepower. The other men, their assistance not needed, stood looking on in grim silence from the scattered provisions and camp equipage. Just as Will drew rein, the groaning vehicle rose, teetered on two wheels, and then bounced hard into an upright position, only to list dramatically to an evidently broken axle.

From left and right, men started toward the sideboard and then stopped, every face going ashen.

The water barrel was in splinters underneath, the sunlight alive in its bent hoops.

From out of the onlookers, an aging, frail figure finally went to the crushed barrel and stooped, drawing a finger across the ground. Even from a distance, it was obvious that the soil had lapped up the water so thoroughly that Ratcliff could find no mud to stir.

Ratcliff straightened and turned, and as he addressed the cowhands, his soft, South-flavored voice had gone raspy.

"We're in some trouble here, boys."

No one had to tell Will. His dry mouth and fiery throat, his cracked lips and burning face, the way he hunched in the saddle and grew faint when he looked up too quickly—one and all, they told him.

Trouble.

Bad trouble.

The chuck box was in shambles, and Hub started for it across ground powdered white with flour and strewn with dried beans and smutty cookware. Rail, seemingly driven, followed close behind, kicking tin plates and cups out of the way. Catching up, he clutched Hub's shoulder and spun him around.

"You seen that storm comin'!" said Rail. "Could've staked the wagon down, you damned cripple!"

Rail drew back his fist—his *left* fist, keeping the gloved hand with the splayed fingers at his side.

"There's three things get a man fired!" shouted Ratcliff. "Gambling, I might put up with. Drinking too, if the time's right. You go starting a fight and you'll walk out of here without a horse!"

The warning was enough for Rail to turn and lower his fist, but exclamations of panic spread like the wildfire into which Will had tried to charge his horse on the divide between the Devils and Middle Concho.

"What do we do now?"

"Sun's bakin' us to a crisp!"

"Got to go back!"

Tommy was abreast on Will's right. Not unsurprisingly, the young man's reaction was the strongest, and he began bouncing in the saddle and flailing his arms.

"Can't take it! Can't take it!"

"Easy, Tommy, my man." From Will's left, Arch's calm voice came from an approaching roan; he had been one of the riders who, from a position beyond the overturned wagon, had righted the vehicle with rope and horsepower.

"Rail done it! Rail done it!" continued Tommy. "He drunk my water! He drunk my water!"

Rail had done so, all right. He had made a point of declaring that he was drinking Tommy's share, and then evidently had tripped the handicapped man to make sure that he would be denied.

Tommy persisted in his rant. "Can't take it! Can't take it!"

"'I beg you, take courage,'" quoted Arch. "'The brave soul can mend even disaster.'"

Will wasn't so sure. But he knew that the juice of canned tomatoes could keep a man alive, and he called hoarsely across camp.

"Hub, how we fixed on airtights? Somethin' to make a difference?"

The *cocinero* turned. "Nothin' that won't make your innards get up on their hind legs cryin' worse for a drink."

For a man under the judgment of the Almighty, Will figured it was the answer he deserved, but that didn't keep him from addressing the Bar X boss.

"How far's next water, Mr. Ratcliff?"

"That would be Howard's Well," said the older man. He winced and began to shudder, and as his jaw tightened and a tic seized his cheek, he seemed unable to find a breath. "They . . . They call it that, anyway. Ought to be Perdition's Well."

It was the second time that Ratcliff had spoken disparagingly of Howard's Well. But Wampus, tugging the stump of his ear from alongside the wagon tongue, didn't give Will time to reflect on it. Wampus seldom kept quiet when there was a complaint to register.

"Ain't what you was asked," he said, paying deference neither to Ratcliff's age nor position. "How the hell far is it?"

In his response, the older man showed restraint; maybe he had used up too much energy in yelling at Rail.

"Already past Johnson's Run, about the halfway point." Ratcliff's words were barely distinguishable. "Forty miles from the Devils to Howard's." He still couldn't say *Howard's* without grimacing.

"So we's closer to Howard's than the Devils?" pressed Wampus.

"I expect. Providing it has water."

"Ain't no time to be guessin'," Wampus grumbled. "Way things is, guess wrong and we's dead."

For once, Will agreed with Wampus. Righteous penance may have descended, but Will still had a mission to fulfill on behalf of Zeke.

Arch took his roan closer to Ratcliff, drawing the man's attention. "You express reservations as to Howard's Well."

"Never could rely on the waterhole, but the well always had water. Never this kind of drouth, though."

"Can't take no chance then," said Hub. "Got to go back where they's sure water."

Ratcliff removed his sweat-stained hat long enough to run fingers through his sparse hair and glanced back toward the Devils River. With his scored face bathed by fierce sunlight, he stared as if deep in thought, and then he turned with a weary sigh to the unknown trail to the west.

"Have a duty to get those cattle to the Pecos," he said, as if to himself.

"Ain't seen no sign of a cow since the duster blowed in," said Wampus. "Horses neither."

"Tracks show them heading on west, not going back," said Ratcliff. "Might've caught a whiff of water ahead."

Cattle and horses both had a nose for water, all right. But Will couldn't help but wonder if his own nose was one for judgment.

"Can't just stand here yappin'," said Wampus. "I'm gettin' on that wore-out horse of mine and goin' one way or the other to a water hole." Starting for several horses secured in scrub mesquites past the wagon tongue, he looked back at Ratcliff with a hard glare that the older man didn't appear to see. "Nobody a-stoppin' me, neither."

It was Wampus's way, stirring up trouble where there wasn't any, and it wasn't lost on Arch.

"Our fair Wampus," he said, "would have a burr under his tail if the Almighty Himself welcomed him to the city of pure gold."

"So which away we goin'?" spoke up Rail. He had withdrawn far enough from Hub so that he was close to Will now. "Ratcliff, you's the boss. Tell me damned straight."

Again, the older man checked in both directions, only to glance down a moment and shake his head. "There's a whole herd of cattle out there, what's left of them, headed Pecos way, at least as far as the first hole of water. My job's to get them on to the river and collect the money for the cows that make it. But this is not the army. Every man needs to decide for himself."

In a Big Dry like this, wisdom demanded that Will turn back to sure water at the Devils. But then Ratcliff added something that changed everything.

"If you don't want to go, leave me an address and I'll see you get your pay."

"Like hell," muttered Rail, so quietly that Ratcliff couldn't have heard. "Old man would be havin' a high ol' time with my money. Ain't lettin' him out of my sight."

Just like that, Rail had decided for Will, who had nothing left but his obligation to Zeke. And to meet it, he would have to ride deeper into hell.

CHAPTER 12

There were six of them, riding a gruesome trail of dead cattle for Howard's Well.

Many carcasses were fresh, only hours old. Others, evidently from the first herd, had bloated after ten days under a pitiless sun. Still more carcasses, putrefying ever since some years-ago drive, were mere parchment drawn over rib cages. Scattered bones from decades past no longer suggested cattle, except for bleached skulls with lizards crawling through the eye sockets.

Will thought that after the Big Drift roundup, he would have been immune to the decay, the stench, the swarming maggots. But there were some things a caring cowhand could never get used to, and finding dead cattle with his outfit's brand was one.

He wondered if he would soon be among them.

From the wrecked chuck wagon, they had struck out in late morning with bedrolls behind their saddles, two parties headed in opposite directions in the hope of reaching water. Several men had turned back for the Devils, leaving Will, Arch, Wampus, and Rail as the only Bar X hands to push on northwest with Ratcliff through country loath to accept the living. And then there was Tommy, representing the Wash Baker outfit, a figure almost too gaunt now to throw a shadow. At first, Tommy had continued to rant about his thirst and the share of water he had been denied, but as the dead cattle mounted under the circling buzzards, a change came over him.

"You let him down again, Tommy, you done let him down again," he bemoaned to himself. "Poor Mr. Wash, you let him down awful bad about his cows."

Will let him talk. With the pangs of conscience that Tommy's presence raised, Will would have preferred to ride apart, but the young man had fallen in on his right. Maybe Will could have dropped off the pace to avoid riding abreast, but he was tired of trying to run from punishment he deserved.

"They's dead, they's ever' one dead," Tommy went on. "'You bring 'em to the Pecos, Tommy,' Mr. Wash says to me. 'You bring 'em ever' one.'"

The slow rhythm of hoofbeats carried the moment for long seconds before Tommy spoke again.

"They's ever' one dead. What could've I did different, Will? I sure let Mr. Wash down."

Tommy had asked, and Will was man enough not to ignore him.

"Dry drive all this way," said Will. "He didn't expect you to strike a rock with a stick and water run out. Same with that duster makin' it all worse. Nobody could've done a thing about it."

For a few paces, that seemed to calm Tommy, for he went quiet. But when the horses flushed several buzzards from a fresh carcass, the young man sobbed more words.

"Poor ol' cows, poor ol' cows. They's eatin' ever' one plum' up, the poor ol' things."

"We started with nearly a thousand head," said Will. "Way they got the trail beat out through these drifts of dirt, figure most of them's still alive."

"You think so, Will? You really think so? You think they still a-goin'?"

"Tracks show it, Tommy." He pointed ahead. "See?"

Tommy looked, and even in profile, his drawn, alkali-caked face seemed hopeful for the first time all day.

"What I got to do, Will? What I got to do to take care of Mr. Wash's stuff?"

As Will listened, he began to feel something besides resentment toward the young man. Of all Ratcliff's cowhands, not a single one had expressed concern for the herd's welfare. Broiled by a sun, sapped of strength, and suffering from dehydration, the drovers had talked only of finding water for themselves. Maybe a life-or-death struggle could do that even to a cowboy—Will had lived through the Big Drift blizzard, after all—but he began to see Tommy in a new light.

"What can I do, Will?" Tommy asked again. "I got to help them poor ol' cows!"

"I wouldn't worry too much," said Will. "Cattle got instincts we don't have."

"Indeed, and well-developed senses," spoke up Arch. He had ridden up on Will's left. "Observe how a thirsty cow curls her upper lip back and displays her teeth. It's part of a process to engage olfactory receptors that alert her to the distant molecule H2O, as formulated by the Italian physicist Amedeo Avogadro."

"Huh?" asked Tommy.

"Think he's sayin' cattle can smell water a long ways," translated Will.

"Six miles," acknowledged Arch, "depending on wind currents."

"We's that close to a water hole?" asked Wampus from behind.

"I would refrain from placing a wager on it," said Arch. "Bear in mind that the lead position was invariably assumed by cattalos every morning. They may have inherited from their bison progenitors the ability to sense water from much greater distances."

Now Wampus echoed Tommy's confusion. "Catta *what*? Pro-generals who? We's gettin' our brains baked, you damned idiot! Fancy talk of yours just makin' my head hurt worser."

Arch winked at Will. "Methinks our friend Wampus echoes the Bard of Avalon, who phrased it, 'Conversation should be pleasant without scurrility.'"

Will didn't know why Arch wasted his energy hoorawing Wampus; maybe his friend knew no other way of coping with a situation so grim. Rail, meanwhile, took a different tack.

"Ratcliff!" Rail called from the rear.

The Bar X boss, riding bowed on his sorrel, was a length ahead of everyone, but his horse seemed as spent as Will's.

"This Howard's Well you's talkin' about," continued Rail. "What say if it's near' dry, ain't enough for the six of us. How we decidin'?"

When Ratcliff didn't respond immediately, Will spoke up. "Don't go wishin' more trouble on us. Got enough already."

"I concur," said Arch. "Considering Sol aflame overhead, it would be self-defeating to both man and steed."

"Who the hell is Steed?" asked Wampus.

Arch looked at Will again and managed a smile. But Rail remained serious.

"Said, 'How we decidin'?'" he asked again.

Tommy started bouncing in the saddle and mumbling about the dipper of water Rail had denied him. Then Ratcliff began to rasp emotional words, and Will quieted the redhead with a gesture and listened.

"The things a man will do. . . The things a man damned has already done . . ."

Now as Will exchanged glances with Arch, neither of them found reason to smile.

"Frankens fell across his mule's neck with the first volley," Ratcliff added quietly, his slow words as pained as any Will had ever heard. "Then Rogers slumped and went down. Jenkins—he was driving the celerity wagon—he whipped those Spanish mules up, the dust flying. I shouldered my shotgun, but my mule was spooked, and I couldn't get a shot.

"Three men, we were, guarding the last Ficklin mail from Mesilla for San Antone, August of '62. Don't know if they were Kiowa or Comanche—both bunches were ranging free, those war years. We made good time from Mesilla to the Pecos, and I was set on getting to San Antone, about to marry. This side of Live Oak, we topped out on the rolling plain and those devils came out of the chaparral on foot, shooting from everywhere."

Ratcliff began to shake. "*The cowards . . . The damned sneaking cowards . . .*"

"Lord A'mighty, Mr. Ratcliff," said Will.

The older man went on, seemingly unaware that his sorrel had halted and everyone was gathered around him.

"My mule got shot out from under me, and I crawled under a cedar bush, there off to itself. I emptied my shotgun fighting those Indians off. Guess they were satisfied when they got the mules, because they disappeared. Come dark, I started walking to Howard's Well, knowing I had to have water, the nearest place.

"A mile down the road, I came upon the mail coach turned over. Moonlight night, almost bright as day. They'd taken the Spanish mules and provisions and cut the mail sack open. Letters were scattered everywhere, white papers glowing in the moon. The driver was lying there dead and scalped in the middle of them."

For a while, no one said a thing, and then from out of the southwest surged a dust devil, whipping Will and forcing him to shield his face. No sooner had it crossed than Rail grumbled again.

"So how's we decidin' who gets to drink?" he pressed. "Settin' here eatin' dust, and ain't heard a answer *yet*, Ratcliff."

Still, the Bar X boss's chin stayed against his chest. "The things a man will do," he whispered again. "The things a man damned has already done . . ."

They were mysterious words, and Will didn't know what to make of them.

As Ratcliff lapsed into silence, Rail urged his chestnut past him. "Y'all stay here and roast. I get to that well first, won't *need* to worry about divvyin' up."

Tommy began to flail his arms. "Will . . . Will . . . he say—"

"Don't worry, Tommy," assured Will. "He push that horse any, he'll be in a worse fix than anybody."

Rail drew rein and looked back, maybe realizing Will was right. The fact was, no one's mount was in decent shape. Will's horse had voluntarily stopped with Ratcliff's sorrel, one of several signs that the Appaloosa was ridden down. For an hour, the Appaloosa's stride had shortened and it had stumbled, despite an ever-slowing walking pace. There had been greater bobbing of its head and neck, and even now, standing still, the horse labored to breathe. Arch had once described a horse as a "fight or flight" animal that would readily comply if a foolish rider pushed it beyond its limits, and Will knew the consequences of being set afoot in country like this.

A rider had to be smart.

Not that Will had displayed anything resembling wisdom today. Indeed, not only did the Appaloosa carry his weight and a thirty-five-pound saddle, but forty or forty-five extra pounds in gold pieces in the money belt hidden around his waist. Miles back, he should have climbed off and walked the horse, but now he had little choice.

"Mr. Ratcliff, Tommy, Arch," he said, naming the only riders he figured would listen, "best we walk these horses a while, don't you think?"

Without waiting for a reply, Will stepped off. He must have been weaker than he had thought, for when he planted his right foot on the ground, his left boot caught in the stirrup long enough to affect his balance. He sprawled, the hundreds of gold pieces in the money belt shifting and clinking.

Damn. The alkali was rising around him, and he could taste it as he rolled to his hip and looked up.

Arch, blazed against the cloudless sky, was staring, his curiosity evident in the lift of an eyebrow. Rail also studied Will, but with suspicion, and more, in his close-set eyes.

"How come you a-rattlin' so, Will?" asked Tommy.

"What you got in them pockets of yours?" quizzed Wampus.

Enough gold pieces to buy a herd wasn't a thing to advertise, and Will didn't know how to answer. His reaction was to say nothing as he dragged himself up by means of the stirrup leather and brushed the dirt off his trousers. He hoped no one would press him, but Tommy wouldn't leave well enough alone.

"Sounded like mister rattle-tail," insisted Tommy. "How come, Will?"

Will looked across the saddle at the redhead. "Better climb off and walk your horse a while, Tommy." It was all that Will could think of to say.

"You went to rattlin' somethin' awful," Tommy went on. "How—?"

Tommy may never have let it go, but Arch came to Will's rescue.

"Tommy, my fine fellow," he interrupted, "dehydration can affect auditory processing. Common sounds become distorted such that they are subject to misinterpretation."

Will didn't know what Arch had said, and he was sure that neither did Tommy nor anyone else. The moment passed without further discussion, and soon the six of them were plodding along on foot and leading their horses.

But not before Will and Arch had exchanged glances.

As he had during the black blizzard, Will clung to Jessie's love as he trudged for minutes or hours, his gait shambling. He stared down as his left boot shuffled forward, then his right, an endless sequence that never let him escape the sun. His headache and lightheadedness grew increasingly worse, and when he finally passed urine, it was dark and foul-smelling. He was quickly losing strength and stamina, and he no longer thought clearly, but a corner of his mind kept whispering three words.

The money belt . . . the money belt . . .

Will had never known how much in gold pieces he carried, but at a typical price of fifteen dollars a head for a fair-sized herd of yearling steers two years ago, it was many thousands of dollars. It was more than a six-bits-a-day cowboy could imagine, and yet Will would have traded every last coin for a dipper of water.

But it wouldn't have been his to trade. Zeke had sent him to bring back the gold to its rightful owner, Andrew Young's widow. Nor would it have been Will's to discard, even though the burden of its weight was more than he could bear. With Zeke climbing the gallows any day now, returning the gold might be the last thing Will could do for the person who had done more for him than any man alive.

The money belt . . . the money belt . . .

The other cowhands knew about it now, but with his thoughts foggy, Will listened to the incessant words a long while before he realized what he had to do. Falling back, he pulled out his concealing shirttail and unbuckled the belt, exposing his chafed skin. At first, Arch alone looked back, obviously checking his welfare. But after Will draped the belt across the Appaloosa and secured it, he found that not only had Rail dropped off the pace, but had twisted around to watch.

As they made eye contact, Rail turned away. When Will stumbled on, leading his horse through rotting carcasses and hideous skulls, his legs felt less dead than before, but now he was troubled by the look Rail had given him.

———

The stress of the moment must have hastened nature's course.

Jessie's first inkling that her time was upon her came only minutes after her revolver's roar had shaken the Pease lowlands. In his lunge for the Colt, Federson had barely avoided the muzzle, but he had fled on horseback with fright in his eyes and bloody pinpricks in his cheek; gunpowder exploding around the cylinder could do that to skin at close quarters. Now, as Jessie remained perched on the cot, she realized that she sat in wet garments and understood that her water had broken.

Jessie had known that this hour was coming, and she and Will had planned accordingly. Nearby were covered cedar buckets, one with drinking water and the other with wash water. In a crate, secured from varmints, awaited salt pork, jerky, and hardtack for the day or two in which she might be unable to cook for herself.

From a chest beside her pillow, she took several rags, as well as shears to sever the umbilical cord, and laid them across Will's bedding. After stripping her cot and remaking it with absorbent linens and a woolen blanket, she added his pillow to her own for the stage in which she would need to prop herself up. From a nail in the corner support post near the wagon swung a lantern; she had filled it the evening before, but she proceeded to trim the wick and add kerosene in case labor extended into the night. Lastly, she removed her wet clothing and washed and dried herself, then slipped on her loosest cotton dress.

With preparations finished, she took up her tally book and pencil and sat waiting for the pains to begin. She was still shaken by Federson and nervous with anticipation, and only one person in the world could help. But all she could do was bare her soul in another letter that no one would ever see.

Will Brite! Will Brite! Where are you? Where? Where!
Don't you know I can't do this by myself?
How come you're not with me?
Why, Will Brite, why aren't you here?

But as she wrote these things, and more, she already knew. She had been forced by man's laws to face her greatest trial alone.

But what of God's laws?

Since her talk with Zeke, Jessie had spent many hours searching for answers in the leather-bound Bible Will had given her. Hadn't Moses married an Ethiopian woman accepted by God? Wasn't the unequal yoking of a believer to a nonbeliever the only marriage that might bring judgment?

Maybe she was about to find out, for she couldn't forget passages that spoke of punishment being passed down to the third or fourth generations for those who hate Him.

"Our baby!" she cried to the sky hidden by the overhead wagon sheet. "Please don't punish our baby!"

In midmorning, the pains began.

At first, Jessie was unsure if they were contractions, for they were mild and passed quickly. She had expected pains in her abdomen, but these extended into her lower back and thighs. Maybe it was just intestinal distress, but the waves came regularly and lasted thirty or sixty seconds at a time, no matter her position.

As the contractions came more quickly and lasted longer, she no longer had doubt.

For hours, Jessie lay panting and sweating and moaning, praying for the baby to come. But something was wrong. Pushing wasn't enough. She called out for Will, but he wasn't there to hear. No one was. She had lighted the lantern while still able, but now sunset was upon her, about to usher in a kind of darkness she had never known before.

CHAPTER 13

"Sixty-two . . . August of sixty-two . . . The things a man damned has already done . . . Sixty-two . . ."

Struggling on, their boot soles dragging when they walked and their torsos arching over saddle horns when they rode, Will and the others inched up a narrowing valley on into dusk. Will was riding abreast of Ratcliff, on the right, when their faltering mounts broke over a summit. Across an undulating plain, he faced an after-sunset sky striking in its beauty but terrifying in the way it glowed orange and red as if the fires of judgment burned just over the horizon.

"Sixty-two . . . August of sixty-two . . ."

Ratcliff had muttered to himself for miles, and he persisted as Will checked him astride the sorrel in the fading light. Will wasn't even sure that the older man was conscious, for his head rose and fell like the nose of his horse. But Arch was very much awake, for his hoarse words came from Will's left as his mount, too, gained the summit.

"As daunting as this transit is on an itinerant cowhand of midthirties, it must represent an ordeal for a gentleman of Ratcliff's years."

"Yeah," agreed Will, only half alert. Letting out a weary breath, he pondered how many more he had left. "I get off this horse, don't know if I could ever get back on."

The truth was, he had never felt this way before, not even in the Big Drift blizzard, and he wondered if this was how a man felt before he died. He seemed a step removed from his body and his heart unaccountably raced, and all he wanted to do was hug the Appaloosa's neck and sleep the long sleep. How easy it would have been to close his eyes to the world and let the inevitable take its course, but he fought the urge yet again, determined to prolong the punishment he had incurred when he had wronged Jessie. Maybe that way he might bear alone the Almighty's judgment so that she and their baby could escape it.

Just past the rim, Will held his horse and waited, not wanting to lose anyone in the coming dark. Arch stopped with him, and so did Ratcliff's sorrel, probably of its own accord. With the pause, Will's Appaloosa began pawing the ground, the instinct of a thirsty horse whose ancestors had dug in mudholes in search of water. Soon, the other three animals had summited and were at a standstill behind them.

"Knowed I should've rid back to the Devils," said Wampus.

Will was in no mood for his complaints. "Nobody was keepin' you from it. Still nobody keepin' you from it."

"Like hell," interjected Rail. "Old man led us ever' one into this. That him still mumblin' to hisself? What kind of man holds our pay over our heads that away, tellin' us ride with him if we want to get it?"

"He said he'd send what you got comin'," reminded Will.

But Rail must not have wanted to hear. "What kind of man?" he asked again.

Will knew, and he thought again of what he and Arch, and even Wampus, had suffered through in chasing after the Slash Five herd in bitter snows that had blinded and claimed toes and ears.

"I'll tell you what kind," said Will, turning in the saddle to find freckled features with crossed eyes and a disfigured mouth that revealed stained teeth. "A honest man. One livin' up to his responsibility. A man like Tommy here."

Will meant every word, but Tommy was clearly too distraught to take pride in hearing it.

"Poor ol' cows, them poor ol' cows," he lamented. "Ain't right, just ain't right them dyin' so. You think they's bedded down somewheres, Will, restin' a spell?"

"Just what I'm fixin' to do," said Wampus. He shifted his weight to his left stirrup in order to swing his far leg over the bedroll behind the cantle.

"I'd think on it first," warned Will.

"What skin is it off *your* nose?" As if in spite, Wampus went ahead and dismounted. "I'll do what I damned well please."

"Suit yourself. Those cattle got better smarts, though." Will turned to Tommy. "Tommy, I don't figure they bedded down at all."

"Indeed," agreed Arch. "In the Big Drift, our bovine friends marched without respite for hundreds of miles to elude a blizzard that would have claimed them. Our fair Wampus is bereft of the instinct of our present charges. It drives them to proceed in the cooler night, lest they expire with the next rising of Sol. As would we."

"What's he sayin', Will?" asked Tommy, who had learned to rely on Will to translate.

"Means we can't last another day in the sun. We got to get to water."

Will squeezed the Appaloosa with his thighs and pushed on, and with him went five horses, including Ratcliff's. A horse was a herd animal, and even with an unresponsive rider, it would go where the others went.

As a hard dark fell and the night wore on, Ratcliff stayed at Will's right, the two of them remaining far enough ahead so that no one else could distinguish the older man's words. Will was astride the Appaloosa and yet he wasn't, the part of him that gave him self-identity seeming to drift away and return in regular cycle. But he wasn't always alone in his purgatory. Jessie was in his arms and yet she wasn't, and from deep in a barred hole, Zeke was looking up at him, and yet he wasn't.

"Sixty-two . . . August of sixty-two . . . The things a man damned has already done . . . Sixty-two . . ."

All that was indisputable was Ratcliff's incessant lament.

And then the Bar X boss began to whisper more of his story from twenty-four years ago. It came in fragments, with no respect for chronology, the babblings of a confused mind haunted by the kind of memories to which Will alone may have been able to relate. Piece by piece, Will fitted Ratcliff's account together, and in the end, it strengthened Will's resolve to cling to life so he could accept even more penance.

Striking out on foot across a waterless land, his companions dead and the sun's quiet fury a greater threat than even the hostiles with their chilling cries and scalp knives, Ratcliff had eventually staggered on raw and bleeding feet into Howard Canyon and found water under a fifteen-foot cliff. Fearing Indians who frequented the springs, he laid up by day in the concealing cedars and beargrass on the slope above and descended for water only at night. A scarecrow of a man in desperate need of sustenance, he survived for a month on the pads of prickly pear and his fading hopes of rescue by a passing party.

Then from his hillside perch one day, he smelled smoke and parted the limbs of his cedar hideaway to see an up-canyon plume from a fire brazenly built, unlike the stealthy practices of Indians. From cedar to cedar, he worked his way along the hillside and dropped down to cliff's edge. Through the upper foliage of green willows, rooted in the drainage below, he looked down on a camp in the brush on the far bank.

Distinguishing a Negro man and woman sitting apart, Ratcliff descended and approached. They were runaway slaves, as thin and bony as anyone he had ever seen. Meat roasted on the fire, and Ratcliff stumbled to it like the starved man he was. He had never tasted bear meat before, and he ate ravenously as the Negro man looked on. The woman, however, kept her face turned away, her chin against her breast. Her demeanor—the fetal-like posture, the tremble, the furtive glances at her companion—led Ratcliff to believe that she was terrified of the man. Nevertheless, both slaves remained tight-lipped in response to his questions.

Gorging himself, Ratcliff rested for hours. Upon eating his fill again, he searched the nearby brush for their bear gun—and found the severed head of a third slave.

The woman's husband.

Brutally murdered.

A cannibalism victim, now shared in by Ratcliff.

Unnatural!

On this night two decades later, the word rolled through Will's mind with all the power of sky fire rocking the earth.

"The things I've done . . ." whispered Ratcliff. "The things a man damned has done . . ."

But that wasn't all that the older man revealed. Surviving because of the ungodly nourishment, he had made his way back to San Antonio and the love of his life, only to learn that cholera had claimed her on the very day that he had found the campfire. Common sense argued for mere coincidence, but Ratcliff knew differently.

It had been punishment from the Almighty for his unknowing complicity.

"A man damned . . . A man damned . . ."

As the older man continued to lament on this night in 1886, it could have been Will's refrain as well for crossing a boundary no man should cross.

God forgive me! Punish me, not her, not the baby!

The only response was the relentless drum of hoofs on a road to death.

CHAPTER 14

Isolated on the Young plantation her entire life, Vennie was unprepared for how the world received her.

For more than two years, she had been a favored member of the Young household, as respected and loved as a daughter. One day, Mistress had invited Vennie's mother into the home, and the moment had been so terrifying that Vennie had hidden under a bed and clung to the springs so that no one could take her away. No matter her reflection in a looking glass, Vennie had stopped thinking of herself as a Negro; she was simply Vennie, and that was enough for her.

But it wasn't for everyone else.

She couldn't stay at Mistress's side even at the train station, for Vennie was confined to a separate waiting area, a cramped and dirty room with a few broken chairs in its shadows. The colored coach was just as miserable, an unclean place where a gruff, white conductor rudely demanded her ticket. After the train was underway, she never saw Mistress even at mealtimes, for coloreds weren't permitted in the dining car at the same time as white passengers. When the train stopped at Fort Worth and a layover was necessary, Vennie had to step down an uncomfortable distance to gravel seared by the sun, while from the regular coach behind, Mistress disembarked onto a covered platform with the aid of a conductor.

It was a world that made Vennie yearn for the plantation cabin that Master Young had promised Zeke and her.

The trip to Wilbarger County took multiple days, with a night or two spent on dingy station benches, but finally a Fort Worth and

Denver City Railway train chugged into Vernon. Mistress acquired a room for herself at a two-story hotel while Vennie waited outside, but colored lodging was more difficult to secure. Fortunately, the clerk directed Mistress across the track to a Negro family, which was all too glad to accept her generous payment to allow Vennie to share a covered sleeping porch with a young daughter.

"We goes to sees him now, Mistress?" pleaded Vennie as soon as accommodations were arranged. "We goes to sees Zeke while we's . . . 'fore he be . . . before they goes and . . . ?"

Hangs him.

Vennie couldn't bring herself to say the words.

"You poor darling, I know your little heart's aching to," said the older woman. "But it's getting late, and there's something we must do first."

Soon Vennie was sliding her hand up the banister of a creaking outside staircase against the sunlit west wall of a mercantile store. At top, Vennie waited on the small platform while Mistress hesitated at a right-side door with a sign:

W. SMITHSON, ATTORNEY-AT-LAW
Please Come In

With a rise of her bosom, Mistress opened the door but stayed in the threshold. Over the woman's shoulder, Vennie could see a man facing them from behind a cluttered desk across a room that smelled of pipe tobacco. At his back were shelves with thick books.

"Mr. Smithson?" asked Mistress.

"Indeed," he said, scooting back his chair with a screech. A heavy-set man with a flushed face, he was sweating profusely despite the open windows.

"I received your telegram," Mistress added.

"Telegram?" Smithson rose and patted his forehead with a handkerchief.

"I'm Mrs. Andrew Young." She glanced back at Vennie. "Do you permit coloreds?"

"Mrs. Young!" Smithson's head drew back in surprise, his eyebrows arching about his widening orbs. "By all means, you're both welcome. You've earned the right."

Vennie followed as Mistress met him halfway and the attorney accepted her hand. If Vennie had learned anything the past couple of days, it was not to proffer her hand to someone white, but Mistress made sure her presence didn't go ignored.

"This is my dear Vennie," said Mistress. "She and Zeke were to be wed." Sadness showed in Mistress's drooping features as she looked back at Vennie a moment. "I pray they are still to be wed."

"I do indeed wish the appellate court had delivered better news," Smithson said quietly. "The fact that Andrew Young's own widow has paid for Mr. Boles's defense is powerful evidence that his conviction should be in question."

Deep emotion came over Mistress, and her voice began to quaver. "It . . . It wouldn't have been in his character, not the Zeke Vennie and I know." She dabbed at the corner of her eye. "He loved and respected Mr. Young. We . . . We need to be certain he's given every chance."

"That, he has had, Mrs. Young, insofar as a colored man on trial for the killing of a white man. I assure you, I mounted as vigorous a defense as I would for anyone. Of course, policy excludes coloreds from serving on a jury. I'm sorry it's come to such a troubling resolution."

"Is there nothing you can do? Money is of no matter."

"I'm sorry. I know of nothing else."

"It wouldn't be too late if someone was brought forward, would it? The man who caused it? The one who really murdered my . . . my . . ." Mistress's words failed her, but nothing could silence her ensuing plea. "*Please* tell me it wouldn't be."

Smithson's eyebrows rose. "Do you have information that I've not been privileged to receive?"

From the pocket of her serge, Mistress withdrew a letter that Vennie recognized as the one from Zeke.

"We've come all this way to bring this," said Mistress, handing it to the attorney. "Zeke says someone by the name of Will Brite went off to bring back the man responsible. You must get a stay of execution until he returns."

Smithson studied the letter. "I know Mr. Brite. He's befriended my client to a degree I would never have expected. Unfortunately, his status with the law, while not as dire as Zeke's, is problematic."

"What do you mean?"

"He could never return to Wilbarger County without being subject to arrest and imprisonment."

"I don't understand."

"As I told Mr. Brite himself only two weeks ago, he's very much his own man, unswayed by law or societal conventions. He's been indicted for miscegenation and would be incarcerated already had he not fled. I'm sorry for the false hopes Mr. Boles raised in the letter, but unless evidence to exonerate him is presented quickly, his fate is in the hands of the Almighty."

Vennie hadn't understood everything, but the abrupt sag of Mistress's shoulders was unmistakable. For a while, the older woman could say nothing, but when Vennie took her hand, she seemed to find new strength.

"Maybe Mr. Brite has returned without anyone's knowledge. Maybe he learned something to make a difference. Maybe he located the man and is on his way to Vernon now."

"That's a heartbreaking number of *maybes*, Mrs. Young. I will, however, appeal directly to the governor and pass along what you've related. He should at least stand ready on the day of execution to transmit a stay should exculpatory evidence present itself."

Then Mistress Young added one last *maybe*. "Maybe Mrs. Brite has had word from her husband."

"I can only offer you the same advice I did Mr. Brite," said Smithson. "Mr. Boles's execution is all but inevitable, and you must prepare yourselves. I would never do anything to raise more false hope. However, if you wish to ask Mr. Brite's wife about these things, I understand that she is great with child in a Pease River camp north of town."

Vennie felt the squeeze of Mistress Young's hand.

"Might you confirm for me," Mistress asked the attorney, "that we can arrange at the wagon yard for use of a buggy?"

CHAPTER 15

The dusk brought more than darkness.

Soaked in sweat, exhausted by her ongoing labor, and so terribly afraid for her baby and herself, Jessie didn't need anything to magnify her time of trial. The pain alone was more than she could bear. But someone was coming, the ominous sounds carrying across the Pease lowlands.

She could hear the clomp of hoofs and rumble of wheels, the squeak of springs and creak of a carriage, and in greater dread than ever, she reached under her pillows for the revolver. She was glad she had reloaded, ensuring that the cylinder had six rounds instead of the standard five, for she might need every one of them.

Federson had come back, and he would kill the baby!

Blinded by the light of the lantern hanging between them, she could distinguish nothing but an open two-seat buggy in the gathering dark, and with both hands she took aim over her bare, upraised thigh.

"Go away!" she yelled, and squeezed the trigger.

The blast rocked her, the bullet whizzing through the hidden silver-seeded sage. She had intentionally shot wide, hoping to turn him away, but she wouldn't waste the next cartridge. If he came closer, she would shoot to kill, and keep shooting until the firing pin snapped against spent casings.

She heard a panicked cry and quick words. "They be shootin'! They be shootin', Mistress!"

"We're two women!" shouted a second voice.

Jessie relaxed her grip on the Colt and scanned the shadows. "Who's out there?"

"Mrs. Brite? Have we come to the right camp?"

But Jessie couldn't answer except to cry out to another sudden contraction.

"Are you all right?" asked the second voice. "Mrs. Brite?"

There was still no way Jessie could respond, for the pain built to a degree of agony unlike any she had faced.

"Mrs. Brite? Mrs. Brite?"

The calls continued.

"I beg you," said the voice, "please don't shoot anymore! We'll come closer if you'll allow. Might you be in labor? I've midwifed on the plantation for years, if I can assist."

Only now did Jessie manage excruciating words. "My baby! Help my baby!"

Jessie laid the revolver aside and saw two figures enter the field of light. One was a middle-aged woman in an ankle-length gray serge with frilly white collar, the other a Negro girl wearing a calico dress with blue spots.

"Bless your heart!" said the woman as she neared. Upon reaching the side of the cot, she took Jessie's sweaty hand between both of hers. "All by yourself, bless your heart!" The woman looked over her shoulder. "Vennie, bring the lantern."

"Yes'm, Mistress. She gonna have herself a fine baby child."

There were so many questions that Jessie wanted to ask, but only one thing mattered. "Help my baby!" she pleaded. "Please help my baby!"

"Let's take a look, darling." The woman moved to Jessie's upraised knee and checked, then watched as the girl brought the lantern. "A little closer, Vennie," she instructed solemnly. "She's bleeding terribly."

Faint and weak, the world slipping away, Jessie closed her eyes against the darkest moment of her life and feared what would

happen to a baby with a father in prison and a mother who had
bled out.

———

Sleep the long sleep . . . the long sleep . . .

Maybe it was time. Maybe it was all Will had left to do. Maybe he
had failed Zeke the way he had failed Jessie, the way he had failed the
Almighty.

In his delirium, Will imagined that he was already prone across
the saddle horn, his face buried in surrender in the Appaloosa's mane.
Against his cheek, he could feel the animal's sweaty foam, moist and
cool and strangely different in smell. When Will moved a little, the
wetness found his lips, and unaccountably, it tasted like mud.

It *was* mud.

Will didn't know how long he had lain at the hoofs of his horse,
but the reins were still in his fist and the Appaloosa, on his right, was
pawing, slurping, pawing more. When Will lifted his head, he found
daylight reflected in a puddle that formed as the forefeet continued to
dig. His lips trembling, he dragged himself closer and submerged his
face alongside the horse's nose.

There were only three inches of water, and the two of them quickly
depleted the supply. But with slack reins, the horse advanced, pawing
instinctively, and Will inched with it and drank at every new puddle.
A horse normally needed ten or fifteen gallons a day, and a few ounces
at a slurp was a slow way to take it in. But the process forced Will to
drink a little at a time, each swallow soothing his roiling stomach
instead of aggravating it, while the mud continued to cool his body
and calm his twitching muscles and runaway pulse.

Alertness slowly returned, and when he could drink no more,
Will rose to an elbow and looked about. The mudhole stretched thirty
yards ahead to green willows that stood against a fifteen-foot cliff at

the base of a low hill, gentle and dotted with cedars of a darker hue. Through the Appaloosa's legs he could see cattle close at hand, vying for water with cattalo and extra saddle horses. In the opposite direction, more animals waded about, a tightly packed herd jostling and watering, but most important at the moment was what he found over his shoulder.

Four men down in the mud.

Three prone, one on his knees.

And all of them drinking from one watery hoofprint or another.

"Arch," said Will, "we been here long?"

The figure on his knees looked up. "Only my faithful steed could say, wherever he may be among the watering bovines. Day had already broken when I found myself bathing in the finest of mud."

"Same with me. Didn't think we'd make it here."

"'I would not spend another such night,'" quoted Arch, "'though t'were to buy a world of happy days.'"

Will sat up, supporting himself with a hand in the mud. "Mr. Ratcliff, you better? Wampus? Tommy?"

Ratcliff raised an arm a little but continued to sprawl. Wampus grunted something about an unpleasant taste. Only Tommy, with the recuperative powers of youth, came to his feet.

"Mr. Wash's cows sure happy now, Will!" he said, grinning through a mask of mud. "'You bring 'em on, Tommy, you bring 'em,' Mr. Wash tells me. We's sure 'nough doin' it, them ol' cows and me. Now they's gettin' good and watered!"

"Think they drunk most of it before we got here," said Will. "But if it's spring-fed, guess more water keeps seepin' up."

Scanning the mesquite chaparral behind Tommy and finding only bedded cattle, Will suddenly panicked.

Quickly he struggled up, widening his view as he steadied himself against the Appaloosa. They were in a canyon a half-mile wide between gray hills with white bands of rock near the summits, some of which rose four hundred feet. In dark recesses, cedars were thick, but elsewhere only green clumps of beargrass sprinkled the rocky slopes.

"Where's Rail?" he asked.

Arch looked about, and so did Tommy and Wampus. Even Ratcliff raised his head.

"We drop him in the night back up the trail?" pressed Will.

"Seen somebody ride off at first light," said Wampus, rising to his knees. "Had a burr under his tail, way he was pushin' that wore-out horse and mumblin' to hisself."

"Where was he goin'?"

"I ain't nobody's wet nurse. Ain't even sure I wasn't dreamin' the whole thing."

Will would have gone closer, but when he took his hand from the Appaloosa, his balance wasn't what it should have been. "What was he sayin'?"

"How the hell would I know? Might've been somethin' about the Pecos. Yeah, that's it, no law west of the Pecos."

Ever since his first days working cattle in the South Texas Brush Country, Will had heard the old adage that there's no law west of the Pecos, and no God west of El Paso. He looked at Arch and knew his friend was thinking the same thing: Rail had grown suspicious, and he had fled toward a no man's land with that gloved hand and its missing digit.

Or maybe that hadn't been Rail's only motivation.

"Will," said Arch, his forehead creasing as he motioned to the Appaloosa, "I do not see your midriff accouterment."

Will didn't understand, and it must have shown.

"Your money belt," said Arch. "It no longer graces your horse."

CHAPTER 16

The last time Will had descended into a hole this deep, an innocent man had been imprisoned in its shadows.

Now, fifteen vertical feet down a narrow set of hewn steps in a crevice in Howard Draw's rock bed, he waited above Arch's shoulder as his kneeling friend dipped water. The small, irregular pool in the rock couldn't have held more than five gallons. But it seemed to maintain a constant level no matter how many empty airtights Arch filled and handed to Will, who in turn passed them to Tommy and Wampus on the stone steps above.

Ratcliff had directed the four of them here after they had helped the struggling man a few hundred yards up the south-trending drainage from the water hole. Now, not far past the west bank, Ratcliff rested in big mesquites and catclaw bushes at a site marked by old fire rings and rusty cans.

"About all we can carry at one time," said Will, accepting from Arch a large, sloshing airtight that once may have held tomatoes. He turned to Tommy and Wampus, two silhouettes against the light above. "Let's take them on over to where Mr. Ratcliff's at."

Will watched the two men disappear over the rim, but stayed where he was. It was cool at bottom, where the sun never reached, and the air was moist and fresh, but more importantly the well offered privacy.

"Rail," Will said simply as he and Arch faced one another.

The word resonated between the rock walls.

"Indeed, our man Rail," Arch agreed.

"He's gettin' away. Damn it, Arch, he's gettin' away."

"He's certainly making an attempt."

Will lowered his head a moment. "Hell of a man I am, the way I've let ever'body down. Should've yanked that glove off first thing and proved it was him. Look at the fix things are in now, with time runnin' out on Zeke."

"I cautioned you before, Will, that Zeke's fate is all but inevitable, regardless of Rail's flight."

Will swore under his breath. "Soon as we climb out, I'm takin' a fresh horse and goin' after him."

"There *are* no fresh horses. Every equine is spent, as are we. They require a full day or more of water and rest—forage, too, should they find such. You and I as well."

"I'm goin', Arch."

"If you feel you must, I'll accompany you, of course. But wisdom must prevail. Rail cannot travel far, if his enfeebled mount can carry him at all. Especially bearing a belt laden with heavy coin."

Will glanced down, a little ashamed that he hadn't told Arch about the gold. "Yeah, that," he acknowledged. "Never did let on to you about it."

"I assumed from the start that the broader span of your waistline stemmed from something other than repeatedly partaking of the fatted calf."

"How come you never said somethin'?"

"I trusted that you would share whatever information you deem of import."

Will proceeded to tell him the full story.

"Money's just money," added Will when he had finished. "Good some ways, I guess. But it causes a lot of bad, too. That jury figured it was reason enough for Zeke to kill Young and for them to see that he hangs for it. And now there's Rail."

"Indeed, the wisest of men once wrote that 'a good name is rather to be chosen than great riches,'" said Arch. "But I implore you, wait until tomorrow to start after him—for the sake of Jessie and your fledgling family if for no other."

Arch's words stung, but no more than Will's eyes abruptly did.

"*Jessie.*" Will almost sobbed the name, and he looked away and hung his head. "Guess there's a lot I hadn't told you."

"I know you're deeply troubled."

"I . . . I don't know if I'll ever see her again. What the law says, I . . . I don't know. Maybe—Maybe it's God's law too."

He went quiet, not sure he could bear thinking about Jessie and the baby, much less speak of them.

Ultimately, Arch broke the long silence.

"Will," he said in a low voice, "I cannot fathom how the law would play a role. But burdened as you are with matters of the day, I'm sorry I made you revisit a situation so distressing."

"It's sure that, all right, Arch." With a deep breath, Will faced him again. "Jessie's father was colored, and I'm in a fix 'cause of it."

Arch squinted in surprise. "Miss Jessie? I never would have suspected."

"Me neither at first."

For a while, Arch rubbed the side of his bristly face. "Did you *knowingly* marry under such circumstances? The criminal code is quite specific. It applies also to a husband who cohabitates once he learns of the wife's lineage."

"Either way, they got me. I knowed about it, back when we was roundin' up the drift herd. Just didn't know the law had a say in us marryin', some big word or such."

"Miscegenation, a matter that's been subject only to selective prosecution."

"Then when the sheriff come out to the Pease, tellin' us the law, Jessie was havin' so much trouble, family way and such, wasn't no way I was leavin' her. Least, not till I didn't have a choice."

"So that's the personal predicament to which you alluded at the Slash Fives."

"Grand jury called me in, but I didn't show. They catch me, I'll go to prison."

Arch looked down and shook his head. "For two years and perhaps five," he acknowledged. "And to cohabitate thereafter would again bring you under penalty of law."

"It . . . It's a hell of a thing, lovin' somebody and . . . and not ever bein' able to . . . to be together no more. And then there's the baby comin' that I'll . . . I'll never get to . . ."

Will could say no more, nor could he see, and he pivoted to climb the steps, only to hesitate at his friend's words.

"Ancestral matters be damned. No angel could have ministered better to me when I was comatose in her care. Would that the two of you had met in New Mexico. The territory repealed its anti-miscegenation statute."

Will wouldn't turn, for he didn't want his friend to see his emotion. But he couldn't hide what was in his voice.

"Man's laws are one thing, Arch. But what about God's?"

He felt Arch's hand on his shoulder.

"'Rest in the Lord, and wait patiently for him,'" Arch quoted solemnly. "A man so physically beleaguered as you cannot hope to understand the Creator's intent. Come with me and make camp. Rest and nourishment will help you face whatever is ahead."

But at this very moment, Rail was stretching out the distance between them as surely as Zeke's time was growing shorter.

If I go listenin' to you and Rail gets away . . .

He better not. He just better not, Arch Brannon.

———

A cow's ear.

Will couldn't imagine why Tommy insisted on having it. But after Arch had cut the throat of a stunned Hereford no longer able to rise, and the men had set about butchering, the redhead had persisted in asking for the appendage until Will had sliced it off. Now, in a modest break in big, twisted mesquites where meat broiled on a rock-rimmed fire a dozen feet away, Will sat exhausted with his back to the drainage and watched Tommy examine the ear.

The five men were spread out, with Tommy seated to his left against the backdrop of an algerita shrub's blue-green leaflets. The young man had to be as famished as anyone, but he seemed more interested in examining the specimen than in eating the skewer of beef across the rock at his boot. The ear had dripped blood all the way to camp, but now it had apparently dried enough for Tommy to reach for his war bag.

"Ain't keepin' that nasty thing, are you?"

Wampus, behind Will and to the left, drew Tommy's attention. The older cowhand was gnawing a hunk of meat, his face as greasy as it was dirty.

"'You sure 'member things good, Tommy,'" recounted the redhead. "Mr. Wash always braggin' on me that away. Bestest memory he ever seen. Lots of goin'-ons, good and bad either one, I keep me somethin' so's I don't forget."

"Our gentleman Tommy's own form of mnemonics," observed Arch from Will's right.

"He got the pneumonia, you say?" asked Wampus.

Will had never heard of mnemonics either, but Wampus had left himself open to hoorawing, and Arch seized the moment.

"Shakespeare opined that one should have more than he showest, and speak less than he knowest. In Wampus's case, I'm not sure that is possible."

Arch had more to say, but Will was too busy studying Tommy's war bag to listen. The cracked leather bulged, and as the young man folded back the flap to insert his latest keepsake, Will wondered how many years of items it held.

But there was something inside that must have troubled Tommy. He began rocking and flailing his arms, distress showing in his face. Ever since they had struck out from the wrecked wagon, the welfare of the cattle had been almost all he could talk about, but now his earlier emotional refrain came again.

"Mean man . . . what he done . . . oh, that mean man, terrible, terrible . . . Big Red, tell him, Tommy, tell Mr. Wash . . . scared, scared to . . . Done rid off, Mr. Wash and that mean man . . . I let him down somethin' awful . . . Poor Mr. Wash . . ."

Will had been unable in the past to get Tommy to discuss his issues, so he didn't respond. Anyway, had Will been any better about sharing what was inside him? How many days had he ridden with Arch before telling him about Jessie?

But it was heartbreaking to hear Tommy sob his fear of finding a crude gravestone scratched with the words *Wash Baker, shot in back.*

As Tommy continued to lament, Will thought he heard Ratcliff speak, and through the rising smoke he looked at the older man sitting six feet past the charred fire ring. His head hanging, Ratcliff listed to his left, seeming to need the support of a rough-barked mesquite at his shoulder. At first, Will couldn't make out what he was saying, but after studying the trembling lips, he was certain he understood.

"The things . . . The things . . . The things a man damned has done . . ."

Will had been there, a boy turned man, haunted by the past. Now he was on the edge of a darkness just as great—and this time he didn't have Jessie to help him through it.

Jessie . . . Jessie . . . !

Will rose and went to Ratcliff, but the Bar X boss didn't seem to know he was there. Indeed, Ratcliff continued to repeat that unsettling phrase.

"You all right, Mr. Ratcliff?" asked Will.

The older man held a skewer of beef, but it appeared to be untouched.

"How come you not eatin'?" Will added.

"A man damned . . . The things he's done . . ."

Ratcliff grew quiet, and for a while the only sound other than Tommy's mutter was the sizzle of grease in the coals. When Ratcliff spoke again, his focus had changed.

"Here . . . Right here . . ."

Will cleared a place among thorny deadfall with his boot and sat beside him. "Plenty of grub. You got to eat, get your strength back."

"Here," continued Ratcliff. "This very spot . . ."

Suddenly Will understood. Shuddering, he checked the ground on his left and then his right, between his upraised knees and over his shoulder. The dirt seemed only that—dirt, scattered with lacy yellow leaves from a previous season—but Will knew it for what it was.

A place desecrated, stained long ago by an ungodly act of which Ratcliff unwittingly had been a part.

"You led us to this spot, Mr. Ratcliff," he said in disbelief. "We passed up better places gettin' here. Why would you do that?"

Ratcliff rested his cheek against the mesquite and clutched the bark, as if it was the only thing to hold onto in life. When his shoulders began to shake, Will knew the answer. Ratcliff was hellbent on destroying himself for violating a boundary that, to his way of thinking, had cost him the love of his life.

Was Will any less guilty?

With Arch jawing with Wampus again, Will had the privacy to speak quietly with the older man.

"You was talkin' in the night. Don't guess you remember."

Ratcliff gave no indication that he heard.

"Don't see how you could blame yourself, her dyin' that way," added Will. His own words rang hollow in his ears, and he gave a half-laugh of disgust. "Guess I'm somebody to talk."

He stood and started away, only to hesitate when Ratcliff spoke.

"I must have said more than I should."

Turning, Will found him still clinging to the mesquite, his face against the bark.

"I know it was tough, losin' her that way," offered Will. "But what went on here didn't have nothin' to do with it."

But as one who had lived through a purifying fire, and maybe was doing so again, Will wasn't so sure.

"What a man damned has done," Ratcliff said again.

"Wasn't no way for you to know, Mr. Ratcliff. Besides, you was nearly dead. *Would've* died. You said so yourself."

"It would have been better. My fault she was taken away. Always wanted a son, but that was taken away too. All my fault."

Will didn't know if that was true or not, but Ratcliff was forcing him to face his own issues in a way he never had before.

"One way or the other, you can always be forgive," said Will. "Friend of mine name of Zeke keeps remindin' me."

It was the second time Will had told that to someone who lived only because of a boundary crossed, and Ratcliff was as unresponsive as Tommy had been.

"Maybe," added Will, "what went on here's the way it was supposed to be, you stayin' alive. The good and the bad, maybe the Good Lord works it so things come out like He wants."

At least that was what Jessie had always told Will. But how could He want *this*, a couple whose love both bound and separated them?

Especially as Jessie faced a woman's most trying hour.

———

A dream world, a nightmare world, and eventually a deep nothingness.

"Mrs. Brite . . . Mrs. Brite . . ."

"Missus . . . Missus . . ."

From out of the nothingness came a pair of distant voices, probing yet soothing, while from nearer rose up a cry as forlorn as it was
yearning. It was that third voice, with its lonely summons, that was
most haunting.

"Will Brite . . . Will Brite . . . Will Brite . . ."

The latter words followed Jessie into awareness, and as she found
herself lying on the cot in daylight, she realized that she spoke them
herself. But she didn't recognize the other voices, although she had a
hazy memory of the two faces above her.

"How are you feeling, hon?" asked the motherly figure who stood
on Jessie's right. "You've had a time, you poor child."

"She be doin' good now, Mistress." On the other side of the cot was
the Negro girl from the same memory. "Yes'm, eyes be wide awake."

All of Jessie's questions from before came back, but only one thing
mattered.

"My baby, my baby."

"Just lie still, hon," pleaded the woman. "He's right here." She
turned and nodded. "Vennie . . ."

Only now did Jessie realize that the girl cradled a bundle in white
linen. At the same instant, Jessie stretched out her arms, driven by
a maternal instinct that surprised her. She took the infant and drew
him close, a new mother amazed by this sleeping miracle of life
with dark, downy hair and a smell so fresh. She knew that it must
be a feeling that comes only once to a mother, and when she touched
her fingers and then her lips to his soft skin, she had never felt so
complete.

And just as powerfully, so alone.

Will Brite, our little boy!

"A fine baby child, Missus," said the girl. "He be stout, loud as he
be cryin', soon's Mistress Young go to smackin' the little thing."

Mistress Young and Vennie.

Jessie had much on her mind, both joyous and mournful, but as she held her baby to her breast, she pondered those familiar names. The Gulf Coast was far away, and yet—

"I'm Mrs. Andrew Young," said the woman with a smile. "This is Vennie with me. I'm so appreciative you wrote us on Zeke's behalf."

"Yes'm," said Vennie. "Be awful obliged."

Jessie had even more questions than before, but her first concern continued to be her baby.

"He's got bruising," she said, kissing the red marks above his eye.

"Oh, that's common, the swelling too, so don't fret," said Mrs. Young.

"He be fine, Missus," said Vennie. "Sucklin' good, whole day long."

Jessie's confusion must have shown in her face.

"You don't remember, do you, hon," said Mrs. Young.

Jessie checked past the woman's gray serge. The long shadows outside the shelter fell in a direction that indicated late afternoon.

"I lost a day," said Jessie.

"You've been through so much since yesterday," said Mrs. Young. Then she glanced at Vennie and her face turned solemn. "Please pardon me if I seem abrupt, Mrs. Brite, but have you word from Mr. Brite?"

Jessie only looked at her, and the woman moved quickly to explain.

"I wouldn't want to bring trouble on such a friend to Zeke as your husband has been. But time is important."

"Yes'm," said Vennie, her chin quaking. "They be fixin' to . . . to hangs . . ."

Jessie knew all too well of Zeke's nearing execution.

Mrs. Young continued. "You wrote us that Mr. Brite went off to bring back the man responsible. We've been hoping, praying, there's news."

There was such pain in the woman's eyes, and in Vennie's long face, that Jessie wished she had something to share. But all she could do was tell them the truth.

"I haven't heard from him. I don't know where he's at." Her eyes welled, and she looked down at the radiant features of the son Will might never see. "He can't come back, not even to . . ."

"Oh, Lord," Mrs. Young whispered.

Her shoulders dropped, but Vennie's reaction was stronger, for she fell sobbing across the other cot.

"Oh, Mistress, Mistress! They be goin' to hangs Zeke! They be goin' to hangs him!"

Mrs. Young brushed her cheek as she went to the girl. "Poor darling, you poor darling," she said, sitting at Vennie's side and stroking the dark hair. "We can't give up. We just can't as long as we have the Lord."

Clearly, these two people from Zeke's past didn't have the bitter hatred for him that he feared. Jessie knew that the kind of deep love she felt for Will Brite—and which Vennie obviously felt for Zeke— could overlook a lot of things. But the response of the widow of the man Zeke had been convicted of murdering was surprising.

"I—I wants to sees him, Mistress!" wailed the girl. "I wants to, I wants to!"

"I know you do, Vennie; I know how much it means to you," consoled Mrs. Young. "But you mustn't let him see you like this. You must be strong."

Through a mist, Jessie kissed her baby's bruises again. With her own emotions so raw, she didn't know where she would find her own strength if God hadn't blessed her with this part of Will.

Will Brite! How could they take you away from me?

"I gots to sees Zeke!" Vennie went on. "Just gots to!"

"Darling," Mrs. Young told her gently, "Mrs. Brite is going to need our help for a while. You need to straighten yourself up so we can look after the two of them." She looked at Jessie. "You must be famished, hon." Then she addressed Vennie again. "Get a cook fire kindled, would you? One of us will need to stay here, but first thing tomorrow I'll arrange for Mr. Smithson to accompany you to the jail."

Vennie began to gain control of her emotions and sat up. "I—I be gettin' the fire goin', yes'm."

The older woman turned and gave Jessie a bittersweet smile. "Before you do, let's find out from Mrs. Brite what she plans to name that precious, precious child."

Vennie wiped her eyes and faced Jessie. "What it goin' to be, Missus?"

Jessie looked again into the angelic face of her sleeping baby and knew there could be only one name.

"Little Will."

But she was crushed to think that he might never know his father.

CHAPTER 17

"How come y'all goin' off, Will? How come? How come?"

All during the time that Will and Arch had roped and saddled fresh horses at the waterhole, Tommy had been a presence in the early morning light. Will had been coy about their plans, but the young man must have overheard enough to suspect that they were quitting the drive. Now, as Will snugged the cinch on a big bay, Tommy stood over him and kept up the questioning.

"What about Mr. Wash's cows, Will? 'You bring 'em on, Tommy,' Mr. Wash says to me, 'you bring 'em to the Pecos.' How I goin' to do it, three of us left? How I goin' to do it?"

Will didn't want to face him. A cowboy had a responsibility to a herd, but he had an even greater obligation to a fellow hand, and someone like Tommy didn't deserve to be abandoned yet again in life.

"Some things me and Arch got to take care of," Will said quietly.

"I help you any, Will? I sure be glad to help you."

Will knew that the young man meant it, and even though the cinch was now secure, Will continued to work with it to delay the inevitable.

"Will?" pressed Tommy. "Let me grab me a horse right quick."

"No, you better stay here."

Will turned to find Tommy distressed, his forehead creased and a spasm in his lower lip.

"You ain't comin' back, you ain't, you ain't," Tommy sobbed in realization. "I'm lettin' Mr. Wash down again, lettin' him down somethin' awful."

"Tommy . . ."

Will didn't know what to say, but the young man did. His bottom lip pushed up. "I ain't your friend no more! I ain't, I ain't, I ain't!"

A screwworm maggot. That's how Tommy made Will feel, for the first time in a long while. Arch must have seen it in Will's face, for he spoke up from the withers of a red dun just beyond the bay's hindquarter.

"You've proven your worth and more, my good man Tommy. By tomorrow, the stronger cattle should be ready to march. The remainder, I fear, are destined for the valley of dry bones. Never underestimate what three of you might accomplish. In 1865, a gentleman named Reynolds—George, I believe—escorted a herd to northern New Mexico with the aid of a mere two associates."

Maybe so, thought Will, but neither of them was Wampus or an aging man beaten down by life.

With a deep breath, Will stepped up on his horse. When Arch raised a hand to Tommy in parting and rode away, Will reined the bay about to follow, only to hesitate. Looking back, he pictured the distraught young man as the doorstep baby shuffled unwanted from family to family until taken in by Wash Baker—a man he would do anything not to disappoint.

"I'm sorry, Tommy," he said. "I'm just . . . sorry."

From the quivering jaw to the glistening eyes, Tommy's hurt and turmoil couldn't have been clearer.

"You ain't sorry! You ain't, you ain't!"

All Will wanted to do was ride away, but he stayed for a moment, accepting the tongue-lashing. Finally, as with that last daybreak with Jessie, he tried to focus on the practical rather than the emotional.

"Whatever you do," he said, "when you get out in that dry country, that sun beatin' down, remember they's just cows. They can be replaced, but Wash Baker can't ever find another you."

Then Will was away on his mission, knowing there could never be another Zeke either.

But Tommy's cry—"I ain't your friend no more, I ain't, I ain't!"—went with him, growing louder with every pace of the bay.

———

What's the use.

For scorching miles up a side canyon trending out of the west-northwest, Will had ridden in silence with Arch on his right. There was only a whisper of wind today, and the dust that kicked up from the hoofs lingered in place. The day before must have been just as calm, for faint horse tracks marked the course ahead. For two men on a trail so old, that, at least, was a godsend.

But Will wondered if everything else in his life had come from a place of judgment.

Yeah, what's the use.

"So my friend's vocal cords are indeed still functional."

Arch's voice shook Will back into the moment at hand. Turning, Will looked at his friend moving against the gray hills studded with green beargrass clumps.

"This dun steed of mine," continued Arch, "doubtless has pondered if my bounteous remarks were intended for him rather than you."

"I go quiet on you?" asked Will. "Guess I'm bad about that."

"If I may inquire, what's the use of *what*?"

"Must've been talkin' and didn't know it. I was just thinkin'—here I go trying to do right by somebody, and I do somebody else wrong."

"Our friend Tommy," acknowledged Arch.

Will looked down at the saddle horn. "I don't know how come life's so twisted up. Things got a way of comin' at you from all directions. What's a man to do."

"The best he can, Will. The best he can."

Arch's unusually serious tone brought Will's gaze up over his bay's ears. The way ahead looked as dark and lonely as all the years behind, except for a too-brief time with Jessie.

"Guess my best wasn't ever good enough," said Will. "It's like I get myself horsewhipped ever' which way I turn. Got it comin', I suppose. Startin' way back, ten years old."

"Unresolved trauma from childhood can indeed destroy a man," said Arch.

"It can do that, all right," agreed Will.

"Case in point . . ."

Will turned, but suddenly his friend seemed to have no inclination to say more. Arch maintained his silence for several paces of the red dun before pulling down his collar.

"If the . . . If the light is proper," said Arch, "you may still detect slight scars." With his finger, he traced out faint markings from below his ear to a point across his throat.

"What is that, Arch? All the times I been around you, never noticed it."

Arch let his collar fall back against his neck. "My stepfather had a peculiar way of repeatedly disciplining a small child. It required the use of a rope, a barn rafter, and a hangman's noose."

"My Lord!"

"My mother eventually fled with me to her family in London. As a consequence, I received the finest of educations, but only in recent years have I come to grips with those early lessons in discipline. My deliverance required, in part, the ear of a friend, a fellow ranger who fought alongside me in the Sierra Diablo snows. You may find that my ear as well is a balm, should you seek it, Will."

For long seconds there were only the overlapping, four-beat walking gaits of the horses.

"It took Jessie and Zeke both," said Will, "but dealin' with things from my boyhood's pretty much behind me now, I guess. There was a awful night back in Texarkana, a shack on our place with a whole family of coloreds livin' in it. 'Better this way,' my old man kept sayin'. 'Ain't slaves of mine no more. Got freed, they did. Can't fend for themselves, and I can't take care of them. Better this way,' he kept sayin'.

"'There on the porch,' he told me, 'get that kerosene poured out.' I knowed better, even when I was doin' it. Soon as he emptied another bucket across the door and shutter, he throwed a match to it all."

Will had unconsciously drawn rein, and the red dun alongside had stopped with him.

"*Sacré bleu!*" exclaimed Arch.

Too much of the old guilt came back, and in self-punishment, Will forced himself to continue facing his friend. "I . . . I can still see that fire, Arch, hear all the screams."

They rode on, two men who had overcome the wounds of their boyhood, and one of them coping anew with a matter that grieved the Almighty. How had the Pease preacher phrased it? That God hates the wicked?

"This stuff with Jessie," Will said eventually. "Keep askin' myself, when's the Almighty had enough of somebody? How much He puttin' up with before He gives up on him? I expect He's thinkin', *Done forgive you once, what you done to those people. Think I'm ever' doin' it again, crossin' the kind of boundary you have*?"

"You mean by marrying Miss Jessie," said Arch.

"Heard a preacher up on the Pease say it. How God put tribes in their own places, and they was to stay there. Unnatural, preacher kept sayin', mixin' colored blood with white."

Arch stroked his bristly chin as he rode without speaking for a long while.

"I would wager," he finally said, "that your man of the cloth finds himself greatly conflicted when he reads of Moses."

"How you mean?" asked Will.

"He wed an Ethiopian lass approved by the Almighty."

"Ethiopian?" repeated Will in surprise. "Isn't that what you call somebody colored?"

"It comes from a Greek compound meaning *burnt face*."

Arch said no more, and as the hoofs proceeded to toll off the seconds of Will's life, he had much to dwell on.

———

The long, steep ascent out of the canyon was another example of why this land was no place to be set afoot.

The loose, whitewashed rocks, blinding as they radiated the sun's merciless rays, fought back against the grinding hoofs of Will's bay. Stumbling and slipping behind Arch's red dun, the bay advanced only slowly, spilling water from the open-topped cans lashed to the saddle. For Will, it was an exhausting ride, but the effect on his horse was even more concerning. He and Arch were already seven miles out of Howard's Well, and next water was a two-day ride ahead.

Down in the dusty canyon, the tracks of Rail's stocking-legged chestnut had told a story of an increasingly faltering horse. How the animal had carried the man this far, Will had no idea. Caution would have demanded that a rider dismount and lead the horse, but the lack of boot prints told Will that caution hadn't been on Rail's mind.

Rail.

He had set everything in motion outside that tavern, and Will had let him get away—maybe for good, from the look of things. Zeke, not Rail, was under the gallows, and if he hung, it would be Will's fault for listening to Arch. So *what* if Will had died out here among all the bones and carcasses? Whom did he have to go back to? The hell with common sense and rest and fresh horses!

"The hell with you too, Arch Brannon."

The instant Will heard himself quietly say it, he regretted it, and when the red dun ahead halted on a brief shoulder of the mountain, he wondered if Arch had overheard. Ashamed, Will didn't want to overtake Arch, much less stop alongside, but when his friend put out his arm, Will had no choice but to draw rein as he came up on the left.

Neither of them spoke. All Will could see were his own glistening hands on the saddle horn. He didn't understand where such a thought had come from, much less how he had muttered it. For a moment, he couldn't have faced even himself in a looking glass, but then he figured this might be part of the penance levied on him. Looking over, he found Arch's intelligent eyes probing.

The quietness lingered, growing more uncomfortable by the second. Arch's slight squint, the contracted brow, the pursed lips cooked by the sun—they painted a picture of a man trying to figure something out. Still, Will wouldn't let himself look away, knowing he had to accept whatever he had coming.

Finally, Arch's chest rose. "I'm concerned, Will," he said quietly.

Just say it. Just say what a ungrateful SOB I am.

But now came the same charged silence, until eventually Arch's gaze fell to the red dun's left shoulder and on below it. Only now did Will notice that the horse stood with a front hoof forward and tipped on edge.

"I feared forequarter distress at the first dip of its nose," said Arch, stepping off. He ran his hand along the animal's shoulder, then lifted the foreleg and checked the hoof. When he lowered it, the dun resumed its unnatural pose.

Pointin', thought Will, recognizing it as a sign of injury. But he had no doubt that Arch's concerns didn't end there, and he stayed quiet as Arch straightened and looked back down into the canyon.

"I have no alternative," said Arch, "but to start back to Howard's Well."

He was right. In the trek back to the waterhole, the lame horse would be tested enough by the empty saddle.

"Do what you want to," said Will.

Even to his own ears, his tone and choice of words sounded callous. Was his resentment for following Arch's advice showing through again?

Taking up the reins close to the bridle, Arch pivoted the horse clockwise in order to descend the mountain. Pausing, he faced Will across the dun's dipping nose. "I regret having to abandon you."

Will knew what he should tell Arch. *Climb up behind me. Let's go get you a good horse.* But he wasn't willing to waste another minute to help the very person at fault for Rail being a full day ahead.

When Will stayed quiet, Arch spoke again. "I'll secure an able mount and follow after you."

The guilt building, Will watched him start down the slope, the surface rocks sloughing to boots and hoofs.

"You still got water, I guess," said Will, trying to appease his conscience.

When Arch found stable footing and looked back, Will reached for a can dangling from the rear housing of his saddle. "Here, take some of mine."

"You have greater need."

Another troubling silence ensued before Will glanced at the scalding sun and studied the canyon floor, barren and unforgiving down and away from Arch.

"Go easy, way this sun is," said Will. This was no spot to leave a man afoot and alone. "Get yourself there in one piece."

"You as well. Wherever 'there' may be for you."

Will, however, wasn't set on reaching a place, but a man. Oddly, he realized his mission wasn't all that different from Tommy's. Indeed, the only thing Tommy wanted to do was deliver the herd to Wash Baker, and Will had all but denied him.

As great as Will's guilt had been before, it was worse now. He was a sorry SOB, all right, living every moment under the judgment of the Almighty and looking to blame someone else for it. Maybe there was no helping him, or Jessie or the baby or Zeke, but if he could do something for Tommy, he might be able to sleep again sometime.

"When you get there," he told Arch, "wait till tomorrow. When the herd's up to it, help Tommy bring them on. I've disappointed enough people."

CHAPTER 18

Its chestnut coat shining in the relentless sun, Rail's horse lay dead on its side with the alkali stirring about the white-stocking foreleg bent at the knee.

For the rest of the day upon parting with Arch, Will had walked and led his bay as much as he had ridden. After a miserable night on the sweltering ground, he had pushed on. Now, near the end of another day, he scared up feasting buzzards and pulled rein before the remains, the worn saddle still in place.

For two days, he had been on a high tableland void of grass but dotted with green cedar shrubs—a land that would have seemed to stretch forever if not for dust devils on the horizon. Not only that, but on all sides the sky came down lower than any place he had ever seen.

Will had never felt so small.

Or alone.

He didn't have Jessie, maybe for the rest of his life, and now he may have alienated Arch. Zeke he might never see again either, but Will had made a promise, and ahead was a drag trail, a cut still deep enough to show despite a whispering wind. It was the kind of mark that a stumbling man might leave if he dragged a belt of gold coin too heavy to carry.

From a burlap sack behind his thigh, Will withdrew the Schofield revolver. As the fluted cylinder and seven-inch barrel glinted in his grip, he followed.

This was it. His long, dark search was all but over. The miles without end in the saddle, the restless nights under uncaring stars, the misery of a boiling sun and raging thirst, the terror of an end-of-the-world storm and an even greater one inside him—they were almost behind him now.

And when they were, he still wouldn't have Jessie.

Jessie! How can I keep goin' without you?

He rode upon a prairie dog town where mounds extended as far as he could see across the bare ground. Before the Big Dry, it must have been home to thousands of the burrowing squirrels, but now the colony seemed lifeless. Indeed, as he traced the line of cattle carcasses through, dodging the holes that could cripple a horse, he found only buzzards and a lone horned toad. Like branded cowhide that could no longer grow hair, this seared tableland was unfit for man or animal.

Not far past the dog town's far edge, he saw a buzzard drop gracefully out of the sky and perch on something low to the ground. The vulture kept its wings spread as it twisted its long neck and warily scouted the scene, but when the wings closed, a host of other buzzards alighted.

With his perspective changing as he neared, Will saw the ground among the stalking scavengers strangely come alive, reflecting sunlight and winking—*glittering like a scattering of gold coins.*

"Hyaah!"

With a cry, Will spurred the bay and the animal bolted. Within moments, he was there, driving the vultures into frenzied flight and pulling rein so hard that the horse almost sat back on its haunches. Before him, a man sprawled belly down, his face turned to his extended right arm and the gloved hand among dozens of twenty-dollar gold pieces that had spilled from the belt.

"Don't you be dead on me!" The dust from the horse's sprint still swept by when Will swung down alongside. "Don't you be dead!"

As he slipped the Schofield inside his waistband and knelt to the clinking coins, he could see only the hangman setting the knot of his rope behind Zeke's left ear. Then Will scanned the shredded back of the shirt and took heart, for dead men didn't bleed, and plenty of blood oozed from wounds inflicted by the hooked beaks.

Will shook him. "Rail!"

When Will got no reaction, he rolled him to his back. The man had lost his hat somewhere and his sunburned face was a fright, his features swollen and blistered to the point that he was almost unrecognizable. Quickly Will retrieved water from the saddle and, lifting Rail's head, dribbled a little between the cracked, puffy lips. Only now did Rail stir, and when the eyelids twitched and opened, Will looked into the black soul of a man who had changed lives forever outside that Big Red tavern.

"MW?" yelled Will. "You're not dyin' *this* easy!"

He poured more water between the lips and checked the area. Through the legs of the bay on his right, Will could see a shrubby cedar twenty yards away. Isolated, the bush cast a dark shadow in stark contrast to the glare of a land blanched by the sun. Will had kept a grip on the reins since dismounting, knowing that a bronc could stray, and he maintained his prudence by leading the animal over and securing it. After returning to Rail, he slipped his hands under the shoulders and dragged him to the shade as the boot heels carved trails.

Will's water was limited, but he dripped a small amount on the man's forehead before helping him drink again. Half-eaten by buzzards and severely dehydrated, Rail was in bad shape, certainly too frail to ride double back to Howard's Well even if Will supported him. Zeke's life hinged on Rail staying alive, and as Will lay back and drew his legs into the shade, he didn't know what to do. Feeling the brush of tiny, blue-green leaves in his face and tasting their resin, he looked up at slivers of bright sky showing through the arbor and weighed his options.

Tomorrow, if all went well, the herd would reach this point. If Rail could rest in the shade and take rationed sips, maybe he could recover enough for Will to get fresh horses and start for Wilbarger County with him.

Wilbarger.

Abruptly, the barrel of the Schofield in his waistband probed Will's abdomen. As he removed it, he realized for the first time the impossibility of sauntering into the very county where a grand jury would have declared him a wanted man. The long weeks and endless miles, the struggles upon struggles—he had been so focused on finding the Schofield's owner that not until now did he consider the consequences to himself.

And just the previous day, he had sworn at the only person who might help.

———

Delirious, Rail woke Will yet again in the night.

Upon deciding the day before to wait for the herd, Will had retrieved the gold pieces and belt and then unsaddled and staked the horse before retreating to the shade again. Still spent from his own ordeal, he had lapsed into sleep immediately and hadn't stirred until after nightfall. He had slept fitfully thereafter, awakening periodically to the feverish man's incoherent mumbling. Now as Will listened, a few reasoned thoughts seemed to pass Rail's lips, not unlike the rambling of Ratcliff on the starlit ride to Howard's Well.

And Rail's words were no less dark.

"Hush . . . Be over quick . . . Quit fightin' . . . You's fightin' me . . . About bit my fingers off . . . Be over quick . . . Seen me . . . This ol' barn . . . Draggin' you . . . They seen me . . . Hush . . . Hush . . ."

Will rose to an elbow, a cedar jag scraping his temple.

"Ain't catchin' me . . . Ain't . . . Ain't . . . San Antone . . . Get to San Antone . . . Nobody find me . . . San Antone . . ."

Will looked at Rail, a mere ghost in the night.

"Violated . . . Hang me . . . Clabberhead girl . . . Went and talked . . . They gonna hang me . . . Newspaper says they gonna hang me . . ."

Will shuddered.

"Keep it . . . Pocket, my pocket . . . No more . . . Don't do it . . . Keep it . . . So's you don't forget . . . No more . . . Don't do it no more . . ."

Just how vile was this man? The pistol-whipping and killing at the tavern, the rape of some girl—how soulless was he?

Will slipped his hand inside the left pocket of Rail's linsey-woolsey shirt and found only cigarette makings, but in the other was something wrapped in ducking. Withdrawing it, Will felt what appeared to be a fold of paper.

Will had to edge out from under the cedar in order to sit up, and when he did, he struck a match to examine what he held. The light flickered on a page from a newspaper, and as he unfolded it with one hand, he could read *San Antonio Express* on the masthead. He had to strike a second match to scan the page, but near the bottom he saw a headline across the second and third columns.

THIN MAN SOUGHT
Feeble-Minded Girl Outraged in Smithville

The match went out, but Will didn't have to read more to know that even the gallows would be too good for Rail.

The sun finally breached the east horizon and burned its way across the sky, and by late in the day, it became clear that Rail was in the midnight of a misspent life. Still, Will did everything he could, repeatedly measuring out water between lips grown silent, until eventually the last can was empty.

Will could already see the dust of the approaching herd through the cedar limbs when Rail breathed his last.

It was over. The looking, the hoping, the praying, it was over. Zeke's fate was sealed, and if Will searched every corner of

Texas—no, of the world, and of the moon and stars and all the things hidden in men's hearts—there would be nothing to change what was to happen.

Zeke would hang by the neck until dead.

———

For days, Zeke had stood on the jailhouse cot and watched through the narrow, barred window as carpenters had worked on the gallows.

The creak of a freight wagon in the open square had drawn his attention first, and he had dragged the cot into place and looked out as laborers had unloaded lumber not far outside. The next morning, two carpenters had arrived, and Zeke quickly had become absorbed by their work.

They began by building a six-by-twelve-foot platform with a pair of apertures eight feet apart. Over corresponding post holes, they constructed a ten-foot-high frame, similar to that for a shed, with cross bracing on all sides. With ropes and mule power, they raised the platform and hammered it into place, then dropped vertical beams through its apertures and on down into the waiting post holes.

The twin beams rose almost eight feet above the scaffold, and when they joined them at top with a stout crosspiece and braced it at the upper corners with angling two-by-fours, the structure took shape. Directly under the crosspiece, the men cut an opening three feet square and fashioned a trapdoor with a ratchet and lever for its release. With the completion of a railing on three sides of the scaffold, the gallows lacked only stairsteps—an even dozen, Zeke heard one of the carpenters say, so that the condemned man would take thirteen steps in climbing to his punishment.

Throughout, they had sawed and hammered from sunrise to dusk, and Zeke had become very much taken by their precision. Now, as he watched them build the staircase under the midday sun, he realized that *this* was the craftsmanship that Master Young would have demanded in overseeing the construction of the home he had promised Vennie and him.

Behind Zeke, the overhead hatch abruptly screeched, and subdued light flooded the jail. *Dinnertime*, he thought as he turned, expecting a rope to lower a burlap sack with hardtack and jerky. Instead, the ladder banged the side of the hatch, and after it dropped with a thud, a shadowy figure began to descend. A flowing skirt told him who it was, and Zeke stepped off the cot and approached.

"Careful, Miss Jessie. Oughtn't be on no ladder, family ways you's in."

But she was much more graceful than before, and when he supported the ladder with one hand and reached up with the other to help her down the final rungs, he saw that her time had already passed.

"Miss Jessie! Boy child? Girl child? Which a one you and Will got now?"

There was something different about her as she gained the shadowy plank floor, and yet never had Zeke known such a familiarity.

"It be me, Zeke. It be me."

That voice, that kind, soothing voice like the gentle flow of Varners Creek on a spring evening . . .

Zeke didn't dare say her name, fearing that to speak it would awaken him from his dream, but when she turned and the overhead light fell across the brown face, he couldn't restrain his whisper.

"Least, I can dream of you. Sweet Vennie, at least I can still dream of you."

But Zeke didn't awaken, and his dream spoke back with a sob.

"I be here, Zeke. I—I be here."

Zeke still may not have believed it, but when the ladder slid up through his hand, the sharp pain of a splinter was all too real. Not only that, but the shout from above was the kind of thing the deputy would have said.

"Don't do no fornicatin' down there. Just like animals, you coloreds."

Then the ladder was gone and the hatch slammed shut, plunging everything into gloom.

"Vennie, sweet Vennie!" Zeke exclaimed. But in the same instant, he drew back, a wretch unfit to be in the same world with her, much less the same room. "Oh, don't hate me! Please don't be hatin' me!"

"How come you's sayin' such? It be me, Zeke, *me*."

When a hand touched his arm, he shrank even more. "Ain't clean!" he cried. "I ain't clean!"

"Ain't you' fault!" Fingers brushed his arm again. "Zeke? Zeke? Jailer man, I expects he don't go lettin' you's wash none."

"Ain't it, Vennie, ain't it at all! I ain't clean inside. Master Young dead, and my hand be on that trigger. Don't hate me, sweet Vennie. Please don't never!"

"But I don't hates you—I don't, I don't! You's be my Zeke, and I be you' Vennie. I loves you!"

Zeke didn't back up any farther, and this time when he felt Vennie's touch, he allowed her inside his arms.

"You come all this ways?" he asked.

"Long ol' train ride, me and Mistress."

Zeke shuddered at the mention of Mistress Young. "Oh, that poor woman," he moaned. "She always so good to this colored person, and now Master Young done gone and it be my fault, my—"

"But you' letters say different. You's say Will Brite fixin' to brings back the man caused Master Young's killin'."

"Will awful good to me too, him and Miss Jessie. But I don't figure I sees Will no more till glory land. Law sure done him wrong, him and Miss Jessie, family ways she in and all."

Vennie clung to him. "Had herself a fine baby child. Mistress be there, midwifin'. Me and her lookin' after Missus Jessie and Li'l Will for a spell."

Li'l Will. If any man deserved to have a son named for him, Zeke knew it was Will. Nevertheless, Zeke had plenty to lament.

"Hatin' me like Mistress Young do," he said quietly, "I reckon she come to watch this colored person dance, end of a rope."

"She tryin' her hardest to *stops* it, Zeke. Way back, she even gots lawyer man to help."

"Mr. Smithson? She the one got Mr. Smithson for me?" Zeke had always wondered which person of means had cared enough to hire the attorney, and to find out that it had been Mistress Young brightened a place in his soul that had been dark for too long.

"You and Mistress Young . . ." Emotion overwhelmed him, and his voice dropped to a whisper. "I—I can goes climbin' them thirteen steps happy now. I can goes to glory land in peace."

Turning, he motioned to the window over the cot.

"They built me a fine hangin' tree, Vennie. Oh, Boss Man up yonder be awful pleased how good they built it, seein' hows it fixin' to send me off to wait for Judgin' Day. I be smilin' now when I show my face, alongside you and Master Young and Mistress, Will and Miss Jessie too, when the Good Lord comes back a-callin' us out of our graves."

Vennie sobbed again. "We . . . We's s'posed be married. We's s'posed be married, Zeke."

"Nobody be married in glory land, preacher men say, but it be better, lots better. I be you' friend, and you be mine, and the Good Lord, He always be a-holdin' us in His hand."

They said more to each other, much more about dreams and disappointments, and about hopes that could be fulfilled only in a far-off land. Zeke would have had the moment last forever, but all too soon, the hatch opened.

"Time's up!" shouted a voice. "Don't want to see you back, neither."

As the ladder dropped and Vennie slipped from his embrace, Zeke couldn't wait for the eternity that he would have with her in glory land.

CHAPTER 19

Will would just as soon have left the body to rot in the sun while the man himself rotted in hell.

If anyone deserved such a fate, it was Rail. But with a flat rock the size of both hands, Will began scooping out a shallow grave in the loosest soil he could find, thirty yards back toward the dog town from the cedar. A proper burial was only right, for the wheeling buzzards dropped lower with every circuit in the sky. It was also right to bury Rail the Christian way, with the feet to the east, and Will was on his knees at the grave's head when he looked down the three-by-six-foot excavation and saw Ratcliff holding point on the far side as the lead cattalos approached.

At ground level, the dust from the flinty hoofs was suffocating, and Will stood and watched the herd pass. The cattalos looked as vigorous as ever, a testament to their hardiness. The power in their shaggy backs and hindquarters showed in their long strides, and if any of them had lost flesh since Pecan Springs, Will could barely tell it. The trailing cattle, meanwhile, could only creep along, an army of skeletons painful to watch.

The herd was strung out for half a mile, the weaker behind the stronger, and even from twenty feet away, Will could feel the generated heat. The lack of adequate drovers had forced the swing men into staggered positions, with Wampus riding by first on the far flank, and a buckskin horse with Arch in the stirrups finally coming up on the near side.

Waiting, Will examined the grave and dwelled on the lonely

miles, the worthless search, the black hood fated from the start to cover Zeke's face in his last moments, no matter his innocence. But in his selfishness, Will also thought of himself. He had been cheated of the only cause he'd had left, and he didn't know how he would take another step.

Lifting his gaze, he saw Arch make eye contact as the buckskin's course brought him closer.

Not his fault. Don't go blamin' him.

Arch veered the buckskin toward him, and Will reminded himself again.

Not his fault.

Arch slowed the horse as he neared.

Don't go blamin' him.

Arch drew rein before Will and studied the grave.

Not his—

"Never should've listened to you," Will heard himself say.

Arch looked up.

Quit it. Don't say nothin' else.

But Will's words kept coming. "Could've caught up with him the first day. He'd still be alive."

Arch had every right to swear at him, just as Will had done at Arch two days ago. Instead, the rider untied a can of water from his saddle and extended it.

Will felt like a scratch-blowing fly, but he took the can and drank sparingly, knowing everyone's supply was limited. When he finished, he chose to stare down at the sky's reflection in the ounces left inside rather than face Arch.

"I took notice of the chestnut's remains back up the trail," said Arch. "Where . . . ?"

Will lifted his eyes and saw him scan the area for Rail's body. "Over at the cedar. Used up all my water. He was too far gone, I guess."

Will tried to give the can back to Arch, but he wouldn't take it.

"You need to rehydrate, Will."

It would have taken a gallon or more, but the few swallows were a salve to Will's raw throat.

"I'll assist you with the body," said Arch, turning his horse toward the cedar.

Still in the grip of emotion instead of logic, Will didn't want his help. "Cattle's liable to stray," he contended.

"Sunset is imminent. Mr. Ratcliff is probably seeking bedding grounds as we speak. He has warned of a treacherous descent that must be navigated in daylight should the herd get wind of water."

Will followed Arch to the cedar and watched him secure the buckskin alongside Will's bay. Upon dragging Rail's body out from under the confining limbs, Will found a hold under the shoulders, and Arch under the knees, and the two of them carried it. With the excavation incomplete, they placed the body outside the grave on the side nearer the herd. Will would have finished out the grave himself, but Arch took up the rock and set to work.

From over his shoulder, Will heard Tommy talking to himself as he came up on drag.

"Poor ol' pony, poor ol' pony. Rail done rid him to death, that poor ol' pony."

Tommy clearly had seen the dead chestnut, and Will was struck again by his sensitivity toward animals. Tommy's lament grew louder, and when a saddle rattled from directly behind, Will knew that he had reined up at the grave.

Will didn't want to face Tommy any more than he had Arch, but he made himself turn and look down Rail's outstretched body at the lathered dapple gray with the young man in the saddle.

"Tommy," he quietly acknowledged.

"How come Rail rid him to death that away? Poor ol' pony, just rid him to death. How come him to do that, Will?"

The dust of the passing herd was settling across Rail's face. "Just wasn't a good man. Least, he won't be treatin' *you* bad no more."

"That Rail, he thought he was a mean'n." Abruptly, Tommy seemed even more distressed. "Didn't know what mean was. I seen mean. Oh, I seen it, seen it somethin' terrible. Should've told Mr. Wash. Poor Mr. Wash."

Will didn't like seeing Tommy upset, but at least he wasn't spewing hatred at him now.

"Looks like you done a bang-up job gettin' those cattle here," said Will, surveying the herd. "Wash Baker's goin' to be proud of you."

"Arch told me, he says, 'Tommy, Will sent me back to help drive them cows.' Says, 'He gone ahead to scout things. He be waitin' for us up aways.' I knowed you wasn't goin' to let me down."

Arch was on his knees in the grave and scraping vigorously, and when Will looked at him and Arch looked back, Will would have welcomed even the esteem of a scratch-blowing fly.

With the grave fully shaped, Arch stepped out and the two of them lowered the body inside. Barely six inches of dirt would cover the remains, a situation made worse by a grave too narrow for a body to lie flat with arms at the sides. Seeking to scrunch the shoulders, Will drew the left arm up across the torso, and then took hold of the gloved right hand.

"What the hell?" he exclaimed.

Will's mind was hundreds of miles away, with a friend doomed to die by a fractured neck or cruel choking, but not so far away that he didn't realize that something was wrong. In the same moment, he yanked the glove off—and found a full five digits.

"It—It's not . . ."

Frantically, he removed the glove from the left hand, once more to find a thumb and four fingers.

He looked up at Arch. "*It's not him!*"

"Indeed, it is not."

Will couldn't digest this. He just *couldn't*. The first thing he could have done upon finding Rail was check his hand, but Will had been so sure, especially after the man had seemingly grown suspicious and fled Howard's Well.

He stood, still trying to understand what this meant. In the meantime, Arch had knelt and was now examining the right hand.

"Note the mangled ring and little fingers," he said. "Rail had indicated a roping mishap, but this has the hallmarks of something else. The scars almost appear to be bite marks."

Meanwhile, Will pivoted in all directions—the high sky and endless flat, the way from which they had come and the fiery horizon with the sinking sun.

"'When He giveth quietness, who then can make trouble,'" quoted Arch. "Whatever Rail's vice or roguery, they have gone with him. His secrecy and mystery will have to endure."

"Maybe not," said Will as he turned. He withdrew the *San Antonio Express* clipping from his pocket and extended it. "Down at the bottom."

Taking the page, Arch unfolded it and began to read. "He had this on his person?" he asked after a full minute. "Given his enigmatic reference to a girl who bore witness against him, I think we now understand his dishonorable treatment of . . ." He glanced at Tommy but didn't say his name. "Too, it relates that she bit his hand severely."

"Never even read that far. Went through a couple of matches just readin' the headlines in the dark. Would've served him right if she'd bit his fingers off."

"Mean man, mean man," Tommy began to rant. "Hand of his bleedin', finger shot plum' off. Awful mean man."

Will looked at Tommy and then at Arch, and once more at the redhead's shaken features. Why had Arch upset him so by telling him what had happened at that tavern?

"All this for nothin'."

In the gathering dusk, Will hunched wearily over a can of water at his bedroll and pondered everything that had happened since he had left Jessie standing forlorn in the daybreak. Beyond the silhouettes of bedded cattle a few hundred yards to Will's left, the sunset sky was still ablaze in reddish-orange, while a few feet before him, Arch smoothed out his own bedroll. Farther away, just out of decent earshot, Tommy sat over his war bag and muttered to himself. Ratcliff and Wampus, meanwhile, were riding first guard around the herd.

"You was right," Will added as he faced Arch. "Zeke's goin' to hang for sure, if he hadn't already."

Arch looked up. "I'm by no means prescient. Any prognostication of mine is mere deduction, subject to myriad variables."

"All the same, you knowed what you was talkin' about."

"I remind you, Will, the remainder of the Bar X employees should be waiting at the Pecos."

"Yeah, but how many hands stay with the same outfit this long? Been over two years since the killin'. I'm ready to give it all up."

Arch's forehead furrowed. "That is not the Will Brite I know."

Will gave a half laugh of disgust. "Guess there's a lot of sides of me I'm showin' that nobody knowed about."

Now there was pain in Arch's eyes. "What I do know is that no man has greater reasons to be troubled."

Will stared at him. He didn't deserve such a friend. He didn't deserve anything but continued judgment from the Almighty for wronging Jessie and their coming child. Embarrassed, he groped for a remark that would turn Arch's attention from him.

"Good to see Mr. Ratcliff up and about," Will said with a glance at the herd.

"Indeed. We've known him only a short while, but he seems a man of high character."

"He'd do to ride the river with, all right," agreed Will. "Wasn't sure, though, but what he planned on dyin' back at Howard's."

Arch seemed to focus even more on Will. "You may be aware of things that I am not. I noticed you deep in conversation with him your last night at camp."

"He's like a lot of us," said Will. "He got down on his hind end and couldn't get up."

"Whatever you discussed with Mr. Ratcliff, it may have had an impact. Upon my return from parting with you, I came upon him off to himself in the brush. He was on his knees with his head bowed, and his hands were clenched together under his chin. I allowed him privacy, but thereafter he acted as if he had discovered new hope."

Now if Will could only find hope of his own to carry him as far as the Pecos.

"Poor ol' things," bemoaned Tommy. "Them poor ol' things."

Astride a gaunt pinto with a rib cage outlined by the rising sun, the redhead was a distraught figure against a backdrop of cattle struggling to rise from the bed grounds. The cattalos were already up, for they rose on their forelegs first—an advantage for a weakened animal, figured Will. But as Will approached on his dark bay, he joined Tommy in mourning the dozens of cattle whose efforts weren't enough.

A cow always lay with knees against the ground, and as she got her hind legs under her, the neck and head would tilt forward, and she would kick out one foreleg and then the other to gain her feet. But these worn-down cattle just didn't have the strength to manage it.

"Can't just ride off and leave them, the poor things," continued Tommy as Will came up alongside. "Maybe if I was to get down and twist their tails."

"I wouldn't even try," said Will. "The ol' sisters are just too weak."

"Mr. Wash sure be disappointed in me, way I lettin' so many die. Oh, I hate it, I hate it."

"Some things can't be helped, son."

From behind came Ratcliff's South-flavored voice, and Will turned with Tommy to see him pulling rein on a dapple gray.

"I've crossed paths with Wash Baker from the San Saba to the Big Red," continued Ratcliff. "He's a fine cowman and a better man. I wasn't along, but I hear we pooled herds with him up the Western Trail to Dodge City in '84."

"Sure done it, we sure done it," Tommy confirmed quietly.

"Anyway, he knew what he was asking of you this trip. Look how many dead cattle we came across from the herd he took. You've done as good a job as he did."

Still, Tommy's eyes were glistening as he surveyed the cattle he would have to leave behind. When Will looked back at the Bar X boss, he saw a lot of sensitivity in his features—the sensitivity of a man who had always wanted a child, but had lost the chance.

"Son," Ratcliff told Tommy after a long pause, "you can't do a thing for them anymore. But the rest of the herd can sure use your help, and so can I."

Tommy turned.

"We've got a thirsty herd, and we're taking the shortest way to water," the older man explained. "Not having a wagon, we can do it. The tableland will go to sloping down, a good hundred feet over the span of half a mile. Then we'll fall off into the head of a narrow canyon, and the bottom will drop out. Lancaster Hill Road, they call it, leading into that wide Pecos valley. You'll be like one of these buzzards swooping down from five hundred feet up.

"There's no place like it I've ever seen, and I'm going to need a couple of good men on point. I want you to be one of them."

Tommy's eyes grew wide. "You mean it? You really mean it? I gettin' to ride point?"

"You bet," said Ratcliff with a smile. "You've earned the right. Now let's get the able cattle headed up so we can move them out."

As Will followed Ratcliff's instructions, he was glad that this caring man hadn't died twenty-four years ago at Howard's Well.

CHAPTER 20

An hour's drive from the bed grounds, the tableland began its gentle drop before the advancing forelegs of Will's horse.

The dark bay carried him along, free of the herd's dust, on right point, while on the other side of the lead cattalos, Tommy rode tall and proudly in matched position. Now that Will observed the crossbreeds stride by stride, he was awed even more by their attributes. All the way from Pecan Springs, the cattalos had held up splendidly, subsisting on scant pasturage and resisting thirst unlike any cattle he had ever seen. He supposed that their buffalo sires had been savage and untamable, but these brutes were about as gentle as milk pen calves.

He couldn't help wondering, however, how manageable they would be when they smelled water after so many days without.

On the herd's far flank, Ratcliff rode up with his horse in a lope and pulled abreast on Tommy's left.

"How you making it?" Ratcliff asked.

"Mr. Wash sure be surprised, me ridin' point," said Tommy.

"Son, it'll put a smile on his face seeing you bring this herd in." When Ratcliff leaned around the redhead, Will could see him better. "We're about to drop off toward the Pecos. Dry as the herd is, they'll pick up the pace when they know water's ahead, especially if there's an updraft when they go down that steep canyon. From the old fort at bottom, it's half a mile on to Live Oak Creek. I imagine it'll be dry, so don't be surprised if they go running south down it to the river, another mile. That's the nearest sure water."

"I doin' good, Mr. Ratcliff?" asked Tommy. "Like Mr. Wash expectin' of me?"

"Wish I had a whole outfit like you. Never knew anybody to care so much about cattle. Horses too. Instead, I've had to hire who I can. That's how I end up with men like Rail and a couple of others."

Suddenly Tommy seemed unable to find a breath. He began to bounce in the saddle, enough to cause the nearest cattalos to shy.

"Easy, son, you're spooking them."

"Mean man, awful mean man," Tommy managed.

"Who's that?"

"Worried sick, worried sick. Him and Mr. Wash rid off together. Mean man, awful mean."

Ratcliff seemed as confused by Tommy as Will was.

"Well, be on your toes from here on out, especially starting down that canyon," the Bar X boss told him. "We'll join up with Wash before you know it. Main thing's to be careful. Used to be a couple of graves down by the fort there, and we don't need any more."

Tommy began to bounce in the saddle again. "*Shot in back, shot in back*, it's goin' to say. Poor Mr. Wash. Oh, that mean man."

"Remember now, don't spook the leaders."

Ratcliff brought his horse around point and pivoted the dapple gray so that he rode alongside Will.

"Didn't mean to upset the kid," he said quietly. "Look out for him, would you? Point's no place for him, with what we've got coming up. But he was so beside himself about those dying cows that I had to do something."

"Means a lot to him," said Will with a glance at Tommy. "He deserves a break or two."

Will anticipated that Ratcliff would drop back to a swing position. But for a moment they had the privacy for Will to pose the question that had been building ever since his talk with Arch the evening before.

"Mr. Ratcliff, been wonderin' if you got any hands up ahead with the initials *MW*."

Ratcliff squinted a little. "Somebody you know?"

"Maybe. Not sure."

Lowering his gaze, the older man rasped his hand across his bristled face.

"Far as the *M* goes, got a lefty by the name of McWhorter," he said, looking up. "Never saw a married man drink so much if you let him. Always figured a good woman would smooth out the rough edges. I was hoping that for myself, anyway."

For a moment, the loss showed in Ratcliff's face. "I dished out powders for McWhorter to ride line down by the Live Oak confluence when they turned the herd loose to graze, so you might run into him there. Not who you're looking for, though. First name's Ike."

When Ratcliff checked the way ahead, he abruptly seemed distracted, but Will followed up with another question anyway.

"There anybody missing a fing—?"

"Sorry, Brite," interrupted Ratcliff. "That narrow canyon's almost on us. Got to get this herd squeezed down before there's a logjam."

Wheeling his horse about, he loped the animal back down the flank.

Will rode on, his mind wandering until he looked across the cattalos' long, ruffled spines and saw Tommy. Despite Ratcliff's warning, the redhead was anything but alert; his paint had swung wide, and cattalos had begun to drift with it.

"Tommy, watch what you're doin'!" Will shouted.

But Tommy had withdrawn the cow's ear from his war bag and now rode hunched over it and muttering.

"Tommy!"

When the young man still didn't respond, Will gigged his bay and circled around the leaders. In moments, he squeezed between Tommy and the straying cattalos.

"What's the matter?" Will asked. With his horse, he began crowding the animals back into the trail. "You got to watch your business."

Tommy, though, seemed lost in whatever memory the cow's ear stirred.

"Not the time to go rememberin' things," Will chided him. One particular cattalo was resistant, forcing Will to use his coiled rope to urge it back into the trace. "Get your mind on your job."

When Will finally faced Tommy, he saw that the leather in his hands wasn't a cow's ear, but a dark-stained glove.

"What you got there?" Will asked. "Put it away, or we're goin' to be in a fix."

"Saw it, saw whole thing," railed Tommy. "Oh, terrible, somethin' terrible, what I seen."

Will studied the way ahead. "Not now. Tell me when we're at camp."

"Big Red, up by Big Red. Just lookin' for Mr. Wash. That's all I was doin', lookin' for Mr. Wash. I come walkin' around the corner and seen it all outside, ever' bit. 'Don't forget, Tommy,' I tells myself, 'Don't never forget this poison joint up by Big Red when y'all was comin' back from that cow drive.'"

Will turned and stared at him. *Poison joint? Big Red? Doans has got just the one tavern.*

"Oh, how that colored man goes to bleedin'," continued Tommy, "way that cowhand beatin' him with a six-gun."

Will's jaw must have dropped. Reaching across, he clutched Tommy's shoulder. "What are you sayin'?"

"Door pops open and here comes a gray-haired man. 'What-the-hell, what-the-hell,' he goes to hollerin'."

Will dug his nails into Tommy's skin. "You was there? You sayin' you was there?"

But Tommy was still in that other time, that other place.

"Oh, what a awful fight they get in, old man and young one. Too stout, way too stout, that young cowhand. Cocks his gun, fixin' to shoot him. Old man just standin' and wobblin', sleepin' with his eyes open. Colored man layin' there all the time, bleedin' terrible, but he grabs that ol' gun, and him and that cowhand go round and round, fightin' over it. Bam! Thing goes off and old man, he falls back and goes slidin' down that post. Oh, that poor, poor soul."

"My Lord! What—"

Will tried, but nothing could keep Tommy from reliving the moment.

"Never seen that the cowhand was wearin' gloves till he come runnin' around the corner. I hid back by a ol' water barrel when he come by, bleedin' and holdin' his hand. Soon's he gets even with me, he yanks off his glove, and one finger's shot plum' off. Crooked Neck sees me and says, 'Go tellin' this and I'll kill you!' Throws his glove down and keeps on runnin'. 'Don't forget, Tommy,' I tells myself. 'Keep it in your war bag so's you don't never forget this poison joint.'"

Dumbstruck, heartened, confused, skeptical—even Arch couldn't have come up with the words to describe what Will was feeling. He didn't think Tommy had a lie in him. But was he simply repeating what Arch might have told him about Zeke?

"Scared, awful scared." The way more words rolled off Tommy's lips in the same rote fashion, he still seemed unaware that Will was alongside. "Too scared to ever say somethin' to Mr. Wash even."

Will focused on the glove. Maybe no other span of leather had ever held such sway over things.

"Can I see it? Can I see it, Tommy?"

He asked multiple times without breaking through Tommy's fog, but when Will reached down and closed his fingers on the glove, the young man let it slide away with no more than a blank look at him.

Stiff and warped, it was a right glove with the ring finger missing. Will looked it over front and back, feeling the rough texture and noting the discoloration that could have been blood. Meanwhile, Tommy said more and Will listened, spellbound, and then Will looked again at the leather and folded back the cuff.

Suddenly something bumped his horse hard, and Will had time only to stuff the glove into Tommy's hand and shout a warning.

"Put it away! We got trouble!"

Whirling, Will found his horse dropping with the leaders into the head of a brushy gulch too narrow for the army of crossbreeds and cattle that pushed from behind. They must have smelled water, for it was the logjam that Ratcliff had feared, an unstoppable flood of hides and horns fighting to squeeze through a rocky ravine no wider than twenty feet. The angling banks on either side were low at first, but they were impossibly steep and covered with scrub cedars with spidery dead branches.

Will had let himself get caught off guard, no matter the justification. Now he and Tommy were in dire straits on the outer edge as their mounts barreled through jagged limbs that gouged and snapped. There was no stopping, no turning back or to the side. With every brutal stride of their horses, the gulch deepened and the bluff at Tommy's shoulder rose higher, and all Will could do was spur the bay ahead so they could ride single file. But the space he created closed quickly, taken up by living skeletons with stampede devils in their eyes.

He couldn't imagine the number of weak animals being trampled.

By the time Will managed a hundred yards to the thunder of hoofbeats, he was wedged between forty-foot bluffs a mere fifteen feet apart. For another 250 yards, the hurtling animals carried him on a curving course to the right, and then Will broke around a two-hundred-foot mountain and the bottom dropped out, just as Ratcliff had described.

From several hundred feet up, Will had a buzzard's-eye view. Framed by the widening canyon walls ahead, the valley of the Pecos unfurled to gray hills eight or nine miles away.

He had only a moment to look, for the surge funneled him down between close-set boulders where the rock peeled the hide from his leg. Will had been on wild rides before—chasing cattle in a midnight run, traversing a torrent of beeves fleeing a winter storm, swimming in mills induced by a blizzard or black duster—but this was a land-slide from which there was no escape.

All he could do was hang on, wondering how much more judg-ment he had coming.

Plenty, maybe, but he had dwelled a lot on what Arch had told him about Moses. From the things Jessie had read to Will, Moses had been someone a man could pattern himself after, and yet Will had learned that this prophet had married an Ethiopian approved by God. Didn't that say something about marrying outside a per-son's race?

He was four hundred feet deep in a gorge now, the cedar slope on the left hiding in shadow and the sparse grass between bands of rock on the right searing in sunlight. The bovines continued to fight for position, jostling the bay. Every so often, Will risked a glance back at Tommy, always finding him a stride behind and his lips moving, as if he constantly encouraged the spooked pinto.

The canyon floor widened, but its twisting drainage stayed treacherous on down to the broad canyon mouth, where the arroyo bore south and the trail veered northwest around the point of a mountain. Finally, the brush was gone and the herd was no longer confined. But the bovines continued their pell-mell drive for water, and Will decided to run with them rather than try to turn the leaders.

He reached the rock foundations and ghostly chimneys of long-abandoned Fort Lancaster, and went west with the herd down a beaten trace. Across a mesquite chaparral flat with punishing thorns, the stampede carried him half a mile to the whitewashed bed of a dry stream. Across it, Will could see a notch where the ongoing trail climbed the bank, but the herd swerved left, cutting off the bay's path so abruptly that the horse piled into a leader and nearly went down.

This had to be Live Oak, and just as Ratcliff had predicted, the herd charged down its bed for the Pecos somewhere ahead. When Will glanced back, Tommy no longer was there, but Will had worries enough of his own. Footing was hazardous and cattalos stumbled and fell, and he couldn't break for the scrub brush on the bank for fear that a hard rein would upend his horse.

Riding only a stride ahead of a shallow grave, Will had every reason to stay focused, but he kept replaying Tommy's words. Upon arriving at Pecan Springs with Wash Baker, Tommy had come face to face with the Bar X rider responsible for the killing. The man had recognized him immediately, for they had ridden with the same pooled herd before their outfits had separated in Kansas for the ride back to Texas.

In the days that had followed on the Devils, anytime Tommy had dared to look at him, the Bar X cowhand had glared back with an unspoken vow.

I'll kill you! I'll kill you! I'll kill you!

Even as Wash Baker and the man had saddled their horses to start away on the drive together, Tommy had stood by, silent and trembling, rather than warn the cowman he virtually worshipped.

Tommy's narrative had been startling. Nevertheless, Will had to be sure that this challenged soul, for whatever reason, hadn't taken Zeke's account for his own. The glove supported Tommy's story, although enough digits were lost in roping accidents that he could have acquired it elsewhere. But it was what Will had found at the last moment, when he had turned back the cuff as trouble had erupted, that was too powerful to explain away.

Just inside, stained by sweat, were printed initials written in ink. *MW.*

And each letter had horseshoe-shaped wings—a perfect match for what was carved into the butt of the Schofield.

Then the bay dropped to its knees in the bed of Live Oak Creek, and the here and now seized Will by the throat as he went over the animal's head.

CHAPTER 21

Some men claimed that stampeding cattle would split and run around a downed rider if given time.

Will wasn't convinced, and he had never known anyone willing to test the notion. If it had been a matter of choosing one death over another, Will would have welcomed a rock to the temple rather than a crush of hoofs. But as with so many things in life, his end wasn't for him to decide.

Before he even felt the blows, the bay's hard skull and the harder gravel were in his face and gone, replaced by flashes of brute shapes and sky and then a swirl of black with specks of light floating through. Maybe all the talk hadn't been a big windy, for he had a vague sense of crawling through flailing forelegs before burying himself behind his fallen horse while cattle stormed by on either side.

When the roar passed and the ground stopped shaking, he could taste the burlap of a sack draped across his eyes. The smell of horse sweat and leather was strong as well, and he scooted away on his shoulder to find chalky dust hanging over the twisted neck of a bay that had given its all.

Will lay facing away from the sun, and thirty yards down the bleached streambed was the watering herd, several hundred animals packed tightly in the shallows of what had to be the Pecos. On across, a bluff sloped up a dozen feet to a haze still drifting across the sky.

"Hell of a wreck."

At the unfamiliar voice, Will rolled over to see the blinding sun winking behind a silhouette that shifted ever so slightly above him.

It was a man, and on his left was the stark outline of a horse against the brightness.

"You hurt?" asked the voice.

Will sat up and assessed his condition. He had plenty of aches, but everything seemed as if it would still work. With the change in angle, he made out the bony features of a cowhand with a thick, angling mustache and chin whiskers. Even though he was about Will's age, the flush in his cheeks and the spider veins in his swollen nose told of someone who had already spent too many years with his spirits. He carried his head cocked, as if he had an injury to his neck.

"You be Ike McWhorter?" asked Will.

"The name they stuck me with."

"I'm Brite." Will checked back past his dead bay and saw empty streambed stretching to a bend. More distant, a couple of miles maybe, the slopes of the tableland lay across the horizon. "Four more of us back there somewhere."

When Will turned again to McWhorter, he noticed that the cowhand held the reins of his roan in a gloved left hand. Suddenly, all Will could hear was Tommy's constant chant all the way from Pecan Springs.

Mean man! Mean man! Mean man!

Will studied the free hand down by the duck trousers. The soiled leather seemed to wrap a full five fingers, and besides, this man's initials were *IM*, not *MW*. But what was it Tommy had said about the person who had fled the Big Red tavern? Hadn't Tommy called him Crooked Neck?

Suddenly everything fit into place.

A Bar X rider with gloves who had gone away with Wash Baker. A pinched neck. And those letters, those tantalizing letters in the butt of a Schofield and inside a blood-stained glove.

M and *W*—not a man's initials, but an abbreviation.

McWhorter.

Will wouldn't do it again. He wouldn't worry about subtlety or propriety. He wouldn't spend another moment in fruitless speculation while Zeke made his final walk to the gallows.

"Feel wobbly as a new foal," said Will. "Could use some help gettin' up." Before McWhorter could respond, Will seized his right hand and squeezed.

Where there should have been a grip four fingers wide, the middle and little fingers folded over one another.

Peering into the bloodshot eyes, Will saw the man for what he was. Almost as an afterthought, he used the maimed hand to pull himself up, but maintained his piercing gaze.

"Obliged," he said, and then he turned to the dead horse and the burlap sack against the rear housing of the saddle.

His pulse pounding, Will reached inside and closed his fingers around sheer steel and textured walnut, only to hesitate and take a few measured breaths.

"Got somethin' of yours," he said.

Withdrawing his hand, he swung and trained the Schofield on a bone button midway down McWhorter's linsey-woolsey shirt.

"You son of a bitch," said Will.

Whether in rage or fear, his voice was quaking. It was the first time he had stood face to face with a man and held a gun on him.

McWhorter's head jerked back. "What the hell? What's this?"

"Recognize it?" Sunlight gleamed in the gunsight. "You got somebody killed with it. There's a man done more for me than anybody. Damned if I'll let him hang in place of you."

"Mr. Wash's cows sure happy now!"

From up the streambed came an exclamation that drew McWhorter's attention, but Will kept his focus on the button down the barrel.

"Tommy?" Will asked in response. "Where is ever'body?"

"Quit runnin' my pony 'fore I come to the—"

Suddenly Tommy must have come close enough to understand what was happening, and who was involved.

"Mean man!" he cried. "Mean man! Mean man!"

"He the one?" asked Will. "This who caused the killin'?"

Rage built in McWhorter's features. "Go to talkin' and I'll kill you!" he warned Tommy.

"Will? Will?" There was terrible fright in the redhead's voice.

Will thumbed back the Schofield's hammer with a *click-click* that brought McWhorter turning quickly, and now his drunkard's face paled and his jaw went slack.

"Will?" continued Tommy. "He say—"

"I heard him, Tommy," said Will. "But *he* just heard me cock this gun, and he's a lot more scared than you are. Go find Arch and bring him. The four of us got some miles to ride."

———

Unnatural!

The circuit rider had shouted the word until it had rocked the banks of the Pease, and for months Will had let the notion drive a wedge between him and the Almighty. Now, as he lashed supplies to his horse and considered the nearby men and stock among scattered boulders in the open flat to the east, he questioned everything the judgmental preacher had said. Indeed, over the course of brutal days in this Big Dry, the Almighty had stepped in again and shown Will things.

Behind him, hidden by the two chuck wagons that had converged on this camp from opposite directions, was the canal-like Pecos, without timber or shrubs to mark its abrupt bank. On the other side, a broad arroyo, spilling down out of six-hundred-foot mountains three miles away, had filled the streambed with gravel and made fording feasible.

Ratcliff called it Pecos Crossing. Arch, who had poured through early army records, said it was Indian Ford. Wash Baker, who had met Will's expectations as a man worthy of Tommy's admiration, knew it as Lancaster Crossing.

By whatever name, the ford was a gateway up the Pecos and on northeast to faraway Wilbarger County. In moments, Will, Arch, Tommy, and their prisoner would strike out with fresh mounts and supplies.

But for now, a quick lesson was in progress. Ever since Will had explained the situation to Baker, the forty-year-old rancher had encouraged Tommy to testify as another step in becoming the man he could be. Tommy, despite his obvious fear of McWhorter, had agreed to do so. Will, in turn, had promised to see to it that Tommy returned safely to Baker's Davis Mountains spread.

With that settled, Baker looked on as his young ward and Ratcliff sat on adjacent boulders and took up their coiled catch-ropes. The smiling Bar X boss proceeded to demonstrate the proper way to throw a loop, and his eager student paid rapt attention. Grazing the sparse grass beyond were twenty cattalos, hardly the worse for wear after a one-hundred-mile march through the most inhospitable country imaginable. Not a single cattalo had perished, while the carcasses of half the full-blooded cattle lined the trail back to Pecan Springs.

All of these—the cattalos, Tommy, and Ratcliff—were in this world only because of unnatural circumstances. They were the products of species interbreeding, incest, or cannibalism, and yet each of them had *worth*, proving that the Almighty worked everything together for good for those who trusted.

And through them, and through Arch's insight, He had shown Will that his union with Jessie had worth as well, no matter man's laws or how loudly a preacher might shout.

But that just made it all the more difficult to accept that they were apart, and might always be.

CHAPTER 22

Vennie had never known the world had such men until she saw for herself.

On a sandbar under the red loam bank of the ribboned Pease, she dipped a cedar bucket in the closest streamlet and felt it grow heavier. Her heart was heavy too this morning, and the gypsum water that filled the pail seemed scarcely wetter than her eyes. Lost, she didn't know what she would do if not for Little Will.

It was essential for a mother and newborn to bond, and Missus Jessie often cuddled and spoke to him even when she wasn't nursing. But with Missus laid up, it had fallen to Vennie to take care of him, and she cherished the moments.

"Baby child be a miracle," she had told Mistress Young. "Yes'm, the Lord's own miracle."

"The world's a strange new place to him, Vennie," Mistress Young had responded. "He's been comfortable and protected, and now he's in a place that's too cold or too hot, and where everything sounds different from before. While he gets used to it, we have to make him feel safe and give him love and attention."

Vennie had been giving him plenty of that. Little Will was so small and in need, and he slept a worrisome amount of time. "To be expected," Mistress had assured her. But whenever he was awake and Vennie picked him up, she seemed to hold a piece of glory land. To a newborn, smiles from a caregiver were important, but smiles came easily when Little Will looked back with eyes that had such striking long lashes.

From day to day, Vennie had seen changes in him. The swelling in his face had gone away, and so had the bruising above his eye. The cone shape of the head had rounded into a normal appearance, and the remnant of umbilical cord had shriveled and darkened on its way to falling off. At first, she hadn't noticed the birthmarks on the eyelids, but now as he slept, she would consider the pleasant rosy tinge.

The yawns, the clench of tiny fists, the way the skin glowed in muted light—Vennie tried to live in the moments, for Zeke was a day away from hanging, and except for Mistress Young, Little Will was all she had.

Well, Little Will and Missus Jessie both.

Vennie had never had a sister, but she would have chosen one like Missus. They had much in common: age, an upbringing in poverty, and, if what the attorney had said was true, Negro heritage. But most of all, each of them was without the person who made her complete.

"How you's does it, Missus?" Vennie had asked one day when Mistress Young was away in town. "How you's gets by a single minute without him?"

She hadn't meant to make Missus Jessie weep, but she had. "It's hard. Awful hard. I—I don't . . . I can't . . ." Then Missus had found a deep breath. "God's hand is stronger than anything life comes at you with."

But that hadn't kept Missus's shoulders from shaking when she had turned away.

In the past, Mistress Young, ever the gracious host, had often entertained, or so she had told Vennie. But Mistress had stopped doing so after Master's death. Vennie supposed it was just too painful to be around guests who couldn't understand her loss, or even worse, who might pity her. But around Missus Jessie, Mistress had rediscovered her outgoing nature, and a relationship of their own had seemed to develop. They talked constantly, and for the first time since the terrible news had come, Vennie saw Mistress Young's smiling eyes return.

"In so short a while, I feel like I have two daughters," Mistress had confided in her.

"A grandbaby too, Mistress?"

"You really love the little thing, don't you, darling."

"Yes'm, seein' hows me and Zeke won't never . . . won't never . . ."

Vennie hadn't been able to say more, but Mistress had understood.

Now, with the morning rays highlighting the sparrows that flitted through the wild plums above, Vennie climbed the bank with a full pail. With Mistress Young still at the hotel, Vennie had temporarily left the baby resting on the cot with Missus Jessie. Once Vennie heated water on the fire, she would have the privilege of giving Little Will a bath.

Topping out, she broke through a shrubby persimmon. A little to the left, dust rose from an approaching open buggy, probably Mistress Young's on the main road from town. Meanwhile, Vennie had a fifty-yard tote ahead of her, and she turned down the thin trail angling to the right through silver-seeded sage grass. Suddenly, through the open shelter's support posts, she glimpsed movement in the pecan mott beyond.

A man was nearing Missus Jessie from behind.

Vennie's first thought was that Will Brite had returned, and her heart began to race with hope for Zeke. But this figure moved furtively from tree to tree, and Vennie had hunted with Mistress Young often enough to recognize stealth when she saw it.

Vennie drew back behind the persimmon. In a few short days, she had learned that the world outside the plantation was a place to tread carefully.

She watched the unkempt man come up unseen and stop just inside the shelter, and an alarmed Missus Jessie go upright and whirl with Little Will in her arms. There were shouts as the man stumbled over the chests that separated them, and a louder uproar as Missus came up with a six-shooter that reflected sunlight. Even before he tore it from her grasp and threw it toward the unhitched wagon, Vennie was running toward them, not even casting aside the sloshing pail in her haste.

"My baby! My baby!"

Missus Jessie's cries were heartbreaking as she struck at the man who tried to take Little Will from her. But they were no more desperate than Vennie's shriek as she broke under the wagon sheet and rushed the man from behind. Swearing and reeking with liquor, he spun with wild red eyes and she swung the bucket by its bail with all her might. The stout cedar smashed into his face, a crushing blow that knocked him back over the chests.

Little Will was crying at the top of his lungs as Missus cradled him protectively, but the man was already stirring in the dirt.

"Missus! Oh, Missus!" Vennie exclaimed.

"Get the gun, Vennie! By the wagon! Get the gun!"

But before she could move, a hand seized her ankle.

"He gots me, Missus! He gots me!"

The struggle seemed to go on forever, Vennie flailing away with the bucket as hands clawed at her from the ground. She was vaguely aware that Missus Jessie had gained her feet and had receded toward the wagon, but the sudden roar of a gun startled her nevertheless.

But no more than it did the man. Releasing Vennie, he scrambled up and fled into the pecans.

"Oh my! Oh my!"

Turning at the cry, Vennie looked past the corner post, where Missus Jessie stood with Little Will, and saw Mistress Young at the wagon wheel, smoke coming from the revolver in her hands. Vennie ran for them, and as they converged, Mistress Young wrapped Vennie and Missus in her arms.

"My girls!" said the older woman as they wept together. "My precious girls and boy!"

Soon, hoofbeats rose up from the mott, and Vennie wasn't alone in turning toward the sound that grew fainter with distance.

"He won't quit," said Missus Jessie. Her voice trembled. "He—He just keeps coming back, after everything he's done."

"Who, dear?" asked Mistress Young.

Missus proceeded to tell a harrowing story of a man named Federson and a fifteen-year-old girl at the mercy of his whims, and of a moment only days ago when he had threatened to dash Little Will against a wagon wheel.

"Oh, you poor child!" consoled Mistress Young. "We have to go tell the authorities!"

But Missus shook her head.

"They won't do anything. Not for me. Not for Will Brite." Little Will had finally calmed, and she looked down and kissed him. "What was it the sheriff said about us? Depraved. That's it, depraved, 'cause white and black don't mix. What . . . What's that make Little Will?"

"Blessed," said Mistress. She looked at Vennie. "You thinking that too, Vennie? That he's blessed to have a mother so sweet as Jessie? And Mr. Brite—oh, the kind things Zeke's said about the both of you."

Then the older woman faced Missus. "Darling, I've lived on a plantation all my life, and coloreds are like family. Take Zeke, the poor thing. Even before he was set free, Mr. Young and I knew he was our brother in the Lord, like Onesimus, and we treated him as such. Society's not ready for intermarrying, same as it wasn't for ending slavery for so long, so they have their laws. But the Good Lord welcomed Moses's Ethiopian wife, and who could ever say Little Will is a mistake?"

Smiling down at him, she smoothed gentle fingers across his hairline. Then her expression turned grave again, and she seemed to study the pecan grove before addressing Missus Jessie once more.

"Jessie, let's get your things gathered. You're going into town and stay with us."

"They won't let me anywhere near the hotel. Not with the talk."

"When we first arrived, I made arrangements for Vennie with a colored family. I'm sure they could accommodate you too." Mistress paused and tapped a finger against her bottom lip, as if deep in thought. "You know we're scheduled to leave on the train tomorrow before . . . before . . ." She glanced at Vennie before continuing. "Jessie, you're such a dear, and Little Will is so precious. I want you to come with us to Brazoria County to live. We have plenty of room in the house and the two of you will have everything you need."

"Oh, please, Missus, please!" urged Vennie.

Jessie's eyes began to well. She glanced back inside the shelter, then at the pecan mott, and finally focused on Little Will.

"Wasn't for the two of you, he . . . he might not even be here." She looked up at Mistress Young. "Having you and Vennie around . . . Growing up, I never made a friend. The man that raised me wouldn't let me. I never had a mother or sister either. But I . . . I don't see how I can go off."

"How come, Missus?" asked Vennie.

"Will Brite. He's going to send for me. One of these days, he's going to send for . . ."

There was no assurance in her voice.

Mistress Young looked the camp over. "We'll leave a note explaining. The Young Plantation, Brazoria County. Don't worry about anyone else knowing. There's enough help at the place to keep you safe. Jessie, you dear thing, you just can't stay around Vernon with that horrid man here."

But even as Vennie reveled in the hope that Missus Jessie would go with them, the world was still a very dark place—and would grow only darker tomorrow.

CHAPTER 23

At sunup on the Pease, McWhorter broke and fled on a roan that was little more than buzzard bait.

For forty miles up the Pecos by mail road, and on up a moat gorged with dead cattle to Horsehead Crossing and northeast across scorched range, McWhorter had done nothing but ride and grumble. With his hands bound to the saddle horn, it was all he could do.

Even after they loaded the horses onto an eastbound T&P train at Midland and took seats in the drovers caboose, McWhorter sat compliantly while the miles rolled by outside the five windows on either side. But he became vocal after Arch, looking over a *Texas Live Stock Journal* issue left behind, read aloud a headline:

HANGING IN WILBARGER COUNTY
Colored Man to Die on 30th

"Might as well cut me loose," McWhorter said. "No way in hell we's gettin' there by then."

Measuring time against distance, Will realized the SOB was right.

"They'll have already hung somebody," continued McWhorter, "and they ain't ever admittin' they got it wrong by arrestin' me."

Will couldn't challenge something indisputable, but he could barely tolerate the man's smug followup.

"Not that I had nothin' to do with it."

All but hopeless, Will and Arch discussed railway connections and schedules with the conductor before deciding the four of them should unload at Sweetwater and strike out on horseback for the still-distant Big Red country to the northeast. Pushing their horses beyond their limits, they traveled day and night, walking and leading the animals only sparingly and sleeping in the stirrups. When their exhausted mounts fell into a feeder trace for the Western Trail on the 29th, McWhorter grew concerned enough to try to intimidate Tommy into not testifying.

"Mr. Wash says, 'You tell 'em, Tommy,'" the redhead responded. "'Show 'em ol' glove you kept and tell 'em what you seen.' I do what Mr. Wash says. He sure a good man. You ain't."

It was an impossible ride, and through a final night the gait of Will's horse grew increasingly stiff. But as Will awoke from dozing in the saddle just before sunrise on the 30th, he found his panting bay moving upstream along a river. The two big mesquites on the left, twisting together on the bank like barber pole stripes . . . the rivulets below, meandering through coppery sandbars . . . the soapberry and mesquite chaparral, blanketing the lowlands beyond . . .

Will recognized the place from the spring roundup.

"Arch, it's the Pease."

"Indeed." Arch rode on Will's left, a little ahead of the roan with the bound McWhorter astride; throughout the night, Will had led the animal by rope. "Twice I've had the pleasure of introducing my bovine charges to its gypsum waters."

"Can't be over seven or eight miles to Vernon," added Will.

"I get to tell 'em soon, Will?" spoke up Tommy from behind. "I sure ready to do what Mr. Wash says."

A cruel reality abruptly struck Will, and he fell silent as his mount crept on for several paces. Finally, he made himself ask.

"What time they . . . they hang somebody, Arch?"

Figuring that Arch knew it was at daybreak, Will wouldn't look at him. He didn't want to judge the sincerity of his friend's answer against what was in his eyes.

"I would think," said Arch, "at whatever time the district judge designates."

Will let the matter go; Arch had allowed Will to keep believing, if only for a little while. But his friend followed up discreetly with another pressing concern.

"Will, you've never indicated, but I presume you want me to escort McWhorter into Vernon."

"Can't ask Tommy to do it."

"Indeed, you cannot, nor could you do so yourself."

Will looked down, flooded by memory, and more so by emotion. "I . . . I've got to see her. This close, I . . . I've got to see Jessie."

There was compassion in Arch's voice when he responded. "With an indictment, the risk would be significant."

"I can't leave here without tryin'. Camp's out of town, on the river couple of miles north."

He heard Arch give a long sigh. "I know what Miss Jessie means to you. Perhaps I could escort her to meet you at an agreed-upon location outside the area."

"She's not able to go anywhere. Havin' a rough time, the baby comin'."

"At the least, I'll plan on riding out and checking her welfare."

But that didn't satisfy Will.

Jessie! Jessie!

The name crawled up from the wellsprings of his soul. What else did he have in this world?

Then he remembered something that Arch had said during their dead man's march, and he struggled for words.

"All . . . All I want is to see her, just . . ." Will faced his friend through a mist. "Case I don't, tell her what you told me."

Arch looked at him, waiting.

"New Mexico," continued Will. "Me and her. A place nobody would bother us."

"Hyahh!"

At the very moment of sunrise, McWhorter's roan had broken between them with a sweeping blow to Will's leg that had rocked his horse. Now, an instant later, the roan was past, a bolt so unexpected that it jerked the rope from his grasp.

"Look out!" Will yelled.

He didn't know if his own mount had a lope left in it, much less a gallop, but McWhorter had kicked the roan into a run. What a man secured to the saddle horn could do if he did escape, Will didn't know, but clods of turf flew from the roan's hoofs and the distance between them was growing. Arch, meanwhile, must have found a trace of vigor in his red dun, for he spurred the animal in pursuit.

Over his mount's poll, Will witnessed it all: the horses' hind limbs reaching ahead furiously, the loud drumbeat as Arch overtook McWhorter, the billowing dust as his friend cut his dun in front of the roan, the crushing collision of men and horses that felled them all with squeals and cries.

"Arch!"

Will was there in moments, swinging off his bay, running between wallowing horses. McWhorter was sprawled, flung out at arms' length from the saddle horn that still held his wrists. Will had never heard such swearing, but Arch may have been incapable of doing so, for he was half-hidden on the other side of his red dun. He could still groan, however, and when Will rushed around the animal's tossing head, he found his friend pinned from the waist down.

"Hang on!" said Will.

But Arch's only response was his continued moan, and Will shouted back up the trail as he stilled the dun by pulling its head to its shoulder.

"Tommy! Bring your horse up here!"

Worrisome seconds followed, but with rope and horsepower and Will's arms under Arch's shoulders, they freed him.

"You broke up?" asked Will.

Arch's face was wrenched as he placed a hand below his side. "'One pain is lessened by another's anguish,'" he managed to quote. "I trust the discomfort of our uncooperative guest exceeds mine."

Will didn't think so; McWhorter and the roan were both on their feet, a cursing man and a horse still bound together at the saddle horn.

"Arch, you able to ride?" asked Will.

"Assist me in rising, if you would be so kind."

Will did his best, and so did Arch, but whatever his injury, his right leg wouldn't support him. Not only that, but when Will dragged him under the shelter of a large mesquite, the pain was too great for him to sit up against the trunk.

"I dare say, my equestrian activity may be curtailed for the moment," said Arch. He looked past Will. "From the appearances of my red dun and the roan, our mode of transportation is equally in doubt."

Will turned and looked. The wreck had crippled both horses, for the roan stood unwilling to put pressure on a foreleg and the dun was unable to rise at all. Weighing his options, Will didn't like what he determined.

Any second now, Zeke would drop through a trapdoor. He would strangle at rope's end, his eyes bulging and his emptying bowels soiling his trousers. Schoolchildren would scream and women would faint, and it wouldn't be over for Zeke as long as his boot heels clicked together. A cruel and undignified death for an innocent man, it was sure to happen, if it hadn't already.

Unless . . .

Will sent Tommy for water while he retrieved Arch's war bag and bedroll from the red dun.

"What are your intentions, Will?" asked Arch.

Will set about making him as comfortable as possible. "Leavin' you grub and plenty of water. Somebody's bound to come along."

"My welfare isn't my concern."

Will called down to the stream. "Tommy! Hurry up!" Then he took the reins of his bay and led it up alongside McWhorter.

"That rid-down horse of yours won't carry the both of us," said McWhorter.

With McWhorter still tied to the roan, Will fed his rope through and around the crossed arms and attached it to itself with a firm knot. Stepping up on his bay, Will measured out ten feet of rope and secured it with a dally around his saddle horn. When he dug out his pocketknife and freed McWhorter from the roan, the man's wrists stayed bound together but his tongue was unfettered.

"No way in hell I'm walkin'."

"Then I'll drag you."

Urging the bay forward, he knew from the slack in the rope that McWhorter trudged along behind.

As Will came even with Arch, he drew rein. "Means a lot, all you done for Zeke."

Now Arch's features showed a different kind of pain. "Will, I don't have to tell you the consequences you face."

Will remembered two troubled riders, of different races, fighting together against a blizzard that had taken their measures as men. He recalled the snow blindness and frozen feet as they had searched for forgiveness for acts that had seemed unforgivable. But most vividly, he lived again the raging heat and black smoke of a wildfire into which he had tried to charge his horse in penance—and would have succeeded, if not for Zeke.

"I owe him my life and more," said Will.

"*Compadre*, our Mexican friends acknowledge in parting who it is that directs our steps, and so will I. Go with God."

For a moment longer, Will held his bay. "Arch, look in on Jessie till I get out."

With Tommy following, he rode on to do what was right and accept his fate.

CHAPTER 24

At daybreak, with the jarring screech of a lever and ratchet, the trap-door of the gallows sprang open.

Zeke had chosen to spend his last night looking up through the small window at the stars he would soon be among. He wondered if Master Young was looking down, waiting to welcome him when the Lord Almighty came back and called them out of their graves. Zeke hadn't seen his departed mother since he had been nine, but she would be there as well, and so would Major Hyler of the Slash Fives, the three of them ready to bare their faces before the true Master. Zeke would join them, another flawed but forgiven individual, and sooner or later so would Vennie and Mistress Young, Will and Miss Jessie.

And all the cruelties of this world would be forgotten.

An hour before first light, the overhead hatch opened and two burlap sacks came down at the end of a rope.

"That fat lawyer says whoever hired him wants you cleaned up," said the deputy. "Water, wash pan, and soap in one, clothes in the other. Don't know who'd care, but arranged with the undertaker too. Ain't buryin' your kind in the cemetery, though. Spot for coloreds outside the fence."

As Zeke untied the bundles and the rope ascended, the jailer had one more remark.

"No use scrubbin' hard. Ain't never gettin' that black off."

Zeke would have wished for a straight razor too, so that he might meet the Almighty clean shaven. But he was moved again by how much Mistress cared for him after everything that had happened. Whiskers or not, he would do her proud, and he proceeded to wash diligently as though rinsing away any sin that remained. If the hangmen kept his body out of the dirt, they could lay him away clean so he would be ready when the Lord Almighty called his name.

Zeke had just slipped into fresh clothes, which he wasn't able to see, when the hatch opened again and the ladder dropped.

"Mr. Boles?" asked an unfamiliar voice as a figure descended.

In all his years, no one had called Zeke *Mister* until his arrest; it had taken a murder charge for a colored man to gain even this token of respect from people he didn't know. But he wasn't bitter, and he met the visitor as the man stepped off the ladder.

"I be here."

"I'm Reverend Bandy. A friend of yours, a Mrs. Young, asked me to attend you."

"Awful nice to me, Mistress Young. I sure 'nough blessed, havin' such good people doin' for me."

The minister and Zeke spent time in prayer, and in talking about the hereafter and what it took to get there. But Zeke knew all about forgiveness, and about committing himself to do right by the Almighty. When the minister placed a hand on his shoulder and they bowed in prayer again, even the sound of the trapdoor springing open outside the window didn't disturb Zeke.

It was daybreak, and the hangman had tested the gallows.

But the minister seemed shaken.

"I've never known a man so calm, Mr. Boles."

"Won't be needin' to hide come that day," said Zeke. "Lord Almighty comin' back, and now I can lets Him see me."

With sunrise, a crowd began to gather outside. Zeke could hear the bustle of buggies and horses, and conversations that became so plentiful that individual voices were lost in the murmur. He hadn't expected this, and he liked to think that people had turned out to pray, and not jeer, as they watched him drop into the arms of the Almighty.

Reverend Bandy kept tugging on his fob and checking his watch, and finally the hatch opened for the last time, and the ladder slid down.

"Get yourself up here, Zeke Boles," said the deputy.

The minister's hand met Zeke's shoulder blade to escort him, but Zeke was on his way to glory land and didn't need prodding. Assured and at peace, he climbed toward the square of sky above, but it was what waited beyond the sky that drew him.

When Zeke stepped out on the flat nook in the roof, the deputy was there to handcuff his wrists behind his back.

"This is what happens when you kill a white man," said the deputy.

As Zeke started down the outside staircase into a cauldron of noise, an abrupt hush fell over the scene, and he saw hundreds, maybe thousands, of faces turn toward him. He had never seen so many people, not even in the Devils River camp for all the cowhands in the roundup of '85. The men and women, crowding the open square on three sides of the gallows, and even the schoolchildren in back, were dressed in their finest, and when Zeke checked his own clothes, he saw that Mistress Young had furnished him with a white shirt and black cutaway coat with matching trousers. He looked so different that he worried that the Lord Almighty might not recognize him when the moment came.

At the bottom of the stairs stood his attorney, dabbing sweat from his face with a handkerchief.

"I failed you, Mr. Boles," said Smithson. "And for that I'm truly sorry."

"Don't fret none," said Zeke. "I be all right, a-headin' for glory land. I sure obliged for all you's done."

With a tight grip on Zeke's arm, the deputy began leading him past the scaffold frame and waiting coffin, the crowd yielding just enough to let them through. Midway across, a bespectacled, gray-bearded man, whom Zeke recognized as the district judge, passed the deputy a sheet of paper. Below the handwriting was a circular green seal that, Zeke supposed, had been attached as a show of authority.

They continued on through cigar and cigarette smoke to the gallows' far side, where Sheriff Lem Hutchins stood before the steps. Upon accepting the document from the deputy, Hutchins looked it over and then motioned Zeke and his escort to ascend. Zeke may not have been able to read, but Master Young had taught him to tally cattle, and he counted off all twelve steps as they creaked under his weight. His thirteenth pace took him to the scaffold, and as the deputy urged him across, he looked back and saw that the sheriff and Reverend Bandy followed.

Zeke could smell the new lumber as the deputy positioned him directly under the braced crosspiece with its dangling noose and turned him toward the east. It was the direction Zeke would have chosen, for the Lord would return like lightning from east to west, and this was good practice for facing Him when he rose from his grave.

Until now, Zeke hadn't noticed that the deputy carried shackles, but they jingled like new spurs as the man fastened them above his boots. Meanwhile, the sheriff went to the railing in front of Zeke and waved the document before the crowd.

"This is the hanging order issued by William Kennedy, judge for the judicial district," he said, in a voice loud enough to carry. Then he began to read:

"'These are therefore to command you to execute the aforesaid judgment and sentence on Monday the 30th of August A.D. 1886, at any time after eight o'clock and before sunset on said day, in the County of Wilbarger, by hanging the said Zeke Boles by the neck until he is dead, and that in said execution, you observe and obey the provisions of the law governing in such cases. Herein fail not, and due return make hereof in accordance with law.'"

Zeke hadn't understood it all, but all he needed to know was the part that said he was to be hanged by the neck until dead.

The sheriff withdrew from the railing, allowing Reverend Bandy to step forward. The minister first offered a prayer, and Zeke was pleased to see every man in the crowd remove his hat and bow his head. After closing with "Amen," Reverend Bandy stayed in place. Back in the jail, he had asked if there was a hymn that Zeke held dear, and so Zeke wasn't surprised when the preacher carried out his wishes by leading everyone in singing the spiritual.

As he listened, Zeke seemed to hear his mother's voice joining in from his boyhood so long ago, and he closed his eyes and pictured the sweet face that he would soon see again.

CHAPTER 25

Steal Away to Jesus.

Years ago, Jessie had found the lyrics tucked in her mother's Bible. But never had they struck her as they did when a thousand voices sang them while Zeke faced her from the gallows across a sea of hats and bonnets prominent in the sun.

There was little room between the crush of vehicles and teams parked along both sides of the square's east frontage road, but Mrs. Young had edged the buggy between the rows and stopped. When she had picked up Jessie and Vennie at their lodging place, Jessie had asked that she drive by the square on their way to the wagon yard and train station. Mrs. Young had resisted on Vennie's account, but after Vennie had promised to hold Little Will and never look up, the older woman had complied.

Jessie would never have been critical of anyone's fragile emotions, but she wanted to be here for Zeke and pray for him. Raised by a cruel man, she knew what it was like not having anyone who cared. Sitting half-hidden in the front seat, she realized that Zeke might never know, but at least she would, and someday, if God was good to her, Will would learn that she had been here for both of them.

Now, the words of the song spoke powerfully of a doomed man's hope for something beyond.

Steal away, steal away,
Steal away to Jesus.
Steal away, steal away home;
I ain't got long to stay here.

Jessie brushed her cheeks as she prayed. Life was short and uncertain, and she and Will could only do their best and hold to the blessed hope of Jesus. With what He had confirmed to her through Mrs. Young, she knew their marriage to be just, no matter man's laws. From the moment they had wedded, the two of them had actually been three, bound together by the highest authority of all and set apart from the world. And with their marriage holy, so was Little Will.

My Lord He calls me,
He calls me by the thunder,
The trumpet sounds within my soul;
I ain't got long to stay here.

Her prayer finished, Jessie looked one last time at Zeke standing ready for the Lord's call, and then she allowed Mrs. Young to drive away down the dusty street. But the singing, and burning eyes, went with Jessie even when the buggy turned left and rumbled through an empty town for the wagon yard and train station.

Green trees are bending;
For sinners set a trembling,
The trumpet sounds within my soul;
I ain't got long to stay here.

———

Jessie may have walked out of Dugan Wagon Yard & Livery while Mrs. Young and Vennie unloaded the buggy, but as she paused in the ruts of the open gate between the plank stables and shielded Little Will from the sun, her mind was still with Zeke.

She wished now that she had let him disclose where Will had gone on his behalf. Once the train chugged out of the station, hidden by the stable on her right, could he ever find her again? Notes were at the mercy of dusters or pack rats, and even if Will located a place for the two of them—three, now that the baby was here—she might never hear from him.

Never!

It was too crushing to think about, especially with Zeke's execution ongoing, and Jessie closed her eyes and considered all the things that she and Will had suffered through to share so little of their lives together. Even if she lasted far into the next century, their year side by side in the crude shelter on the Pease would be the one she cherished.

Hold me. One more time, so I can remember.

Just before he had ridden away, fleeing the coming day and all the injustice, she had whispered the words and accepted his embrace a final time. Now if she could only cling to that memory, of holding and being held, for the rest of her life.

Jessie heard hoofbeats coming down the street, and she opened her eyes to see the nose of a horse nodding into view past the corner of the stable on her right. If someone had come for the hanging, he was too late.

The rider slowly emerged—an undernourished figure bent in sleep or exhaustion over the saddle horn, his bristly face drawn and dusty. Stunned, she tried to say a name but the words wouldn't come, and she rushed into the street to find him leading a shuffling man by rope while another horseman followed at a distance.

Then the rider in front wearily lifted his head, and suddenly he was bolt upright and pulling rein.

"Jessie!"

She looked left and right, checking the street. "What are you doing here! Will Brite, you can't just—"

"Lord, Jessie! I never thought I'd—" Then he evidently realized what she cradled. "The baby? What you've been through!"

"You can't be out like this! They indicted you!"

He glanced over his shoulder. "I've got the man, Jessie. The one that did it, caused the killin'."

"They're hanging Zeke now! The square—right now!"

There was only time for her to brush his extended hand before he twisted around and shouted at the disheveled man at the end of the rope.

"Go to runnin'!"

"The hell with you," growled the man.

Will gigged the bay and the animal jumped forward and jerked the man down.

"Get up and run!" he said again.

Spitting dirt, the man got to his feet. As he broke into a stumbling run to keep up with the bay and the second rider who had come abreast, Jessie spun to Mrs. Young and Vennie in the gate.

"Get the buggy!"

CHAPTER 26

A man with a glinting badge was already adjusting a hangman's knot against Zeke's black-hooded head when Will broke past the jailhouse and saw the gallows across hundreds of hats and bonnets.

The executioner would spring the trapdoor at any instant, and Will knew only one way he might delay it. Reaching back, he found the Schofield inside its burlap sack and thumbed back the hammer as he withdrew it. With the muzzle to the sky, he squeezed the trigger, a blast that spooked his horse and turned every head in his direction.

In a town with an ordinance against carrying firearms, the gunshot had an effect. As he lowered the forty-five and reined the horse into the crowd, not only did startled people give way, but revolvers flashed sunlight from the scaffold.

Will may have ridden into a gauntlet, but he didn't go alone. With him went faces like Zeke's, guiltless faces straight out of the Texarkana night when a ten-year-old boy had helped take away so many futures. Will had found forgiveness, but now he had a chance to carry out the kind of righteous act that they never would because of him.

"Here's the man caused the killin', and somebody that seen it!" Will shouted.

"He's a damned liar!" said McWhorter. "Somebody cut me loose!"

With Tommy following, Will led his prisoner right up below the scaffold and saw a pair of revolvers trained down on him.

"Throw the gun down!" ordered Sheriff Hutchins.

"It's evidence!" said Will. From the jailhouse stairs, a heavyset man was approaching, and when he came within arm's reach, Will passed him the Schofield butt-first. "Tommy Blackburn here watched the whole thing, Mr. Smithson. He's got a glove from the killin' you need to have too."

"Oh, what a awful thing I seen him do!" confirmed Tommy. "Mean man, awful mean McWhorter is!"

Will pulled out his shirttail. "Somethin' else." Removing the money belt, he gave it to the attorney. "Goes to Andrew Young's widow."

"Don't you move, Brite!" The sheriff was coming down the gallows steps. "Off of that horse!"

The moment Will dismounted, Hutchins was there to spin him around and push him up against the animal.

"Hell of a nerve, you've got," said the sheriff, searching him. "Don't think for a minute you're stopping a hanging *this* easy."

Smithson began protesting, but from across the saddle, a man Will recognized as the presiding judge at Zeke's trial spoke up.

"In light of the circumstances, Sheriff Hutchins, I cannot allow the execution to proceed until these claims are examined. I'm rescinding the hanging order pending notification to the governor."

"Doesn't get you off the hook, Brite," said the sheriff as he allowed Will to face him. "I've got a warrant for your arrest. I-god, you and that colored girl's depraved."

"Whatever you got to do. Just get the noose off of Zeke's neck. Then take a wagon seven, eight miles up the river. There's a hurt man layin' there."

"Mr. Brite," said Smithson, showing Will the respect that the sheriff did not, "an innocent man should never hang. If what you and Mr. Blackburn say is true, you've done a great service not only to Mr. Boles, but to our judicial system. But, I fear, at a considerable personal cost to you."

"Some things a person's just got to do."

"Will Brite! Will Brite!"

Will turned to see Jessie pushing her way through the crowd. She would have rushed into his arms, but the sheriff stopped her with an extended palm. Now, for the first time, Will had a chance to marvel at the tiny life bundled in her arms.

"He, or she?" he asked with a smile.

Jessie's eyes were welling. "Little Will."

"He doin' all right?"

She nodded with a bittersweet smile.

"A boy!" said Will, strangely happier than he had ever been in his life. "*Our* boy, healthy and all, the Good Lord's way of approvin' you and me. Jessie, I got a place for us, out in New Mexico, but you've got to wait till I get out."

Then Will began to worry, and his own eyes misted.

"How . . . How will you get by, just you and him?"

"Vennie's here, and so is Mrs. Young from Brazoria County."

"Zeke's Vennie? Is that Andrew Young's widow?"

"Mrs. Young wants me to go stay with her. She couldn't be any nicer to me." She looked at their baby. "To Little Will either."

"Enough of this," said Hutchins.

Taking Will's arm, he turned him away. But he couldn't keep Will from hearing the very words that had carried him through so many trials since that last morning on the Pease.

"I love you, Will Brite."

Down the gallows steps, free of his black fabric hood and shackles, came Zeke, escorted by the deputy. Leading him alongside the scaffold supports, the officer couldn't resist making a snide remark as he approached Will.

"Told you I was savin' a place for you."

Then for a moment, a white cowboy and a Black one, their lives entwined, were allowed to stand face to face.

"Sure good seein' you, Will," said Zeke. "But how come you's doin' this?"

"You've done more for me than any man there is."

"But now they be lockin' you up. Ought've let me gone on to glory land."

Will placed a caring hand on Zeke's shoulder, the way he had done when Zeke had saved him from a fiery end.

"We'll both go there, Zeke, but not till He's ready for us. Figure there's more He's needin' us to do first."

THE END

AUTHOR'S NOTE

Across the land in 1885 swept an insidious blight, showing no mercy.

The "Big Dry" came in the wake of the previous winter's Big Drift, the greatest migration of cattle in western annals. This new pestilence threatened not only much of Texas, but northern Mexico, southern Arizona, and eastern New Mexico. As the drought lingered, the region drained by the Devils and Pecos rivers of Texas became a corner of hell.

"You could have gone up the Pecos River on both sides and it was four feet high with dead cattle," said Frank Lloyd. Indeed, lamented fellow cowhand W. E. McClendon, its waters "smelled terrible and was full of hair and maggots."

By May 1886, when a correspondent from Big Spring, Texas, crossed the area by train, conditions away from the rivers had become equally unbearable.

"The plains west of here," the correspondent wrote, "are parched and dry, and the carcasses of thousands of cattle are to be seen in every direction. . . . The stench as one passes along the Texas Pacific west of here is terrible."

Festering in a cloudless sky, the dead cattle lay like monuments to nature's sovereignty, testing the mettle of anyone who dared the land.

"I thought my eyes would go out from the glare," recalled Mrs. J. H. Barron of Midland, Texas. "There was not a cloud to be seen, nothing but the broiling sun. Everything was parched, and only the bear grass was green."

More than two million cattle had ranged in the drought-stricken area of Texas. In 1884 they had been worth thirty dollars a head. By 1887, a cowman was fortunate to find a taker at four dollars, if any of his beeves survived. In the Pecos country alone, fully 50 percent of the cattle perished.

But the human toll was greater, for the inferno inside a person could burn hotter than any sun.

"The two years drouth of 1886 and 1887," remembered cowhand Walter C. Cochran, "broke all the little cowmen on the Pecos."

SELECTED SOURCES
FOR THIS NOVEL

ANTI-MISCEGENATION LAWS

Paschal, George W. *A Digest of the Laws of Texas: Containing the Laws in Force, and the Repealed Laws on Which Rights Rest.* 4th ed., vol. 1, Houston: E. H. Cushing, 1875.

The Penal Code of the State of Texas Passed by the Sixteenth Legislature February 21, 1879. Austin: State Printing Office, 1887.

COWBOY LIFE

Dearen, Patrick. *The Last of the Old-Time Cowboys.* Plano, Texas: Republic of Texas Press, 1998.

———. *Saddling Up Anyway: The Dangerous Lives of Old-Time Cowboys.* 2nd ed. Guilford, Connecticut: TwoDot, 2018.

DROUGHT OF 1885-1887

Dearen, Patrick. *A Cowboy of the Pecos.* 2nd ed. Guilford, Connecticut: Lone Star Books, 2017.

———. *Devils River: Treacherous Twin to the Pecos, 1535–1900.* Fort Worth: Texas Christian University Press, 2011.

———. *Halff of Texas: Merchant Rancher of the Old West.* Austin, Texas: Eakin Press, 2000.

WILBARGER COUNTY, TEXAS

Jones, Sylvia, ed. *Wilbarger County, Texas: 1858–1986.* Lubbock, Texas: Wilbarger County Historical Commission, 1986.

The New Handbook of Texas, Volume 6. Austin: The Texas State Historical Association, 1996.

ABOUT THE AUTHOR

Inducted into the Texas Literary Hall of Fame, **PATRICK DEAREN** is author of eighteen novels and ten nonfiction books. His writing has been honored by Western Writers of America and several other organizations. A ragtime pianist and backpacking enthusiast, he makes his home with his wife Mary in Midland, Texas. See patrickdearen.com for more information.

Printed in the USA
CPSIA information can be obtained
at www.ICGtesting.com
CBHW030039051124
16919CB00003B/142